THE KNOCKOUT

A KROYDON HILLS LEGACY NOVEL

PLAYING TO WIN
BOOK THREE

BELLA MATTHEWS

Copyright © 2024

Bella Matthews

All rights reserved. No part of this publication may be reproduced or transmitted by any means, electronic, mechanical, photocopying, recording or otherwise, without the prior permission of the publisher, except in the case of brief quotation embodied in the critical reviews and certain other noncommercial uses permitted by copyright law.

Without in any way limiting the author's exclusive rights under copyright, any use of this publication to "train" generative artificial intelligence (AI) technologies to generate text is expressly prohibited. The author reserves all rights to license uses of this work for generative AI training and development of machine learning language models.

This is a work of fiction, created without use of AI technology. Resemblance to actual persons, things, living or dead, locales or events is entirely coincidental. The author acknowledges the trademark status and trademark owners of various products referenced in this work of fiction, which have been used without permission. The publication/use of these trademarks is not authorized, associated with, or sponsored by the trademark owners.

This book contains mature themes and is only suitable for 18+ readers.

Editor: Dena Mastrogiovanni, Red Pen Editing

Cover Designer: Sarah Sentz, Enchanting Romance Designs

Photographer: Michelle Lancaster

Model: Eric Taylor Guilmette

Interior Formatting: Brianna Cooper

SENSITIVE CONTENT

This book contains sensitive content that could be triggering.
Please see my website for a full list.

WWW.AUTHORBELLAMATTHEWS.COM

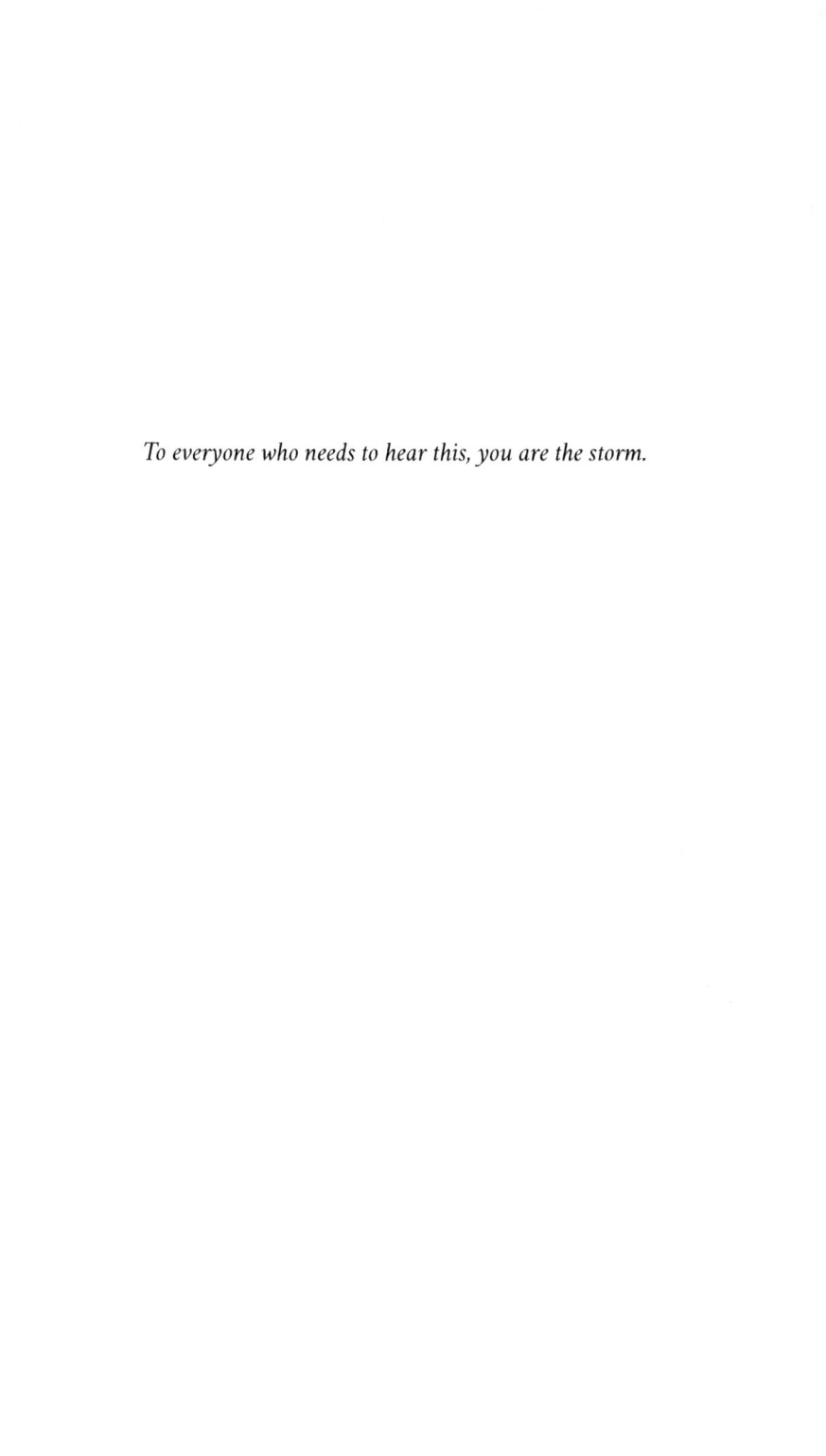

To everyone who needs to hear this, you are the storm.

"Fate whispers to the warrior, 'You cannot withstand the storm.'
The warrior whispers back, 'I am the storm,'"

— UNKNOWN

CAST OF CHARACTERS

The Kings Of Kroydon Hills Family

- **Declan & Annabelle Sinclair**
  - Everly Sinclair - 24
  - Grace Sinclair - 24
  - Nixon Sinclair - 23
  - Leo Sinclair - 22
  - Hendrix Sinclair - 19

- **Brady & Nattie Ryan**
  - Noah Ryan - 21
  - Lilah Ryan - 21
  - Dillan Ryan - 18
  - Asher Ryan - 12

- **Aiden & Sabrina Murphy**
  - Jameson Murphy -21
  - Finn Murphy - 18

- **Bash & Lenny Beneventi**
  - Maverick Beneventi - 21
  - Ryker Beneventi - 19

- **Cooper & Carys Sinclair**
  - Lincoln Sinclair - 14
  - Lochlan Sinclair - 14
  - Lexie Sinclair - 14

- **Coach Joe & Catherine Sinclair**
  - Callen Sinclair - 24

The Kingston Family

- **Ashlyn & Brandon Dixon**
    - Madeline Kingston - 25
    - Raven Dixon - 9

- **Max & Daphne Kingston**
    - Serena Kingston - 18

- **Scarlet & Cade St. James**
    - Brynlee St. James - 24
    - Killian St. James - 22
    - Olivia St. James - 20

- **Becket & Juliette Kingston**
    - Easton Hayes - 29
    - Kenzie Hayes - 23
    - Blaise Kingston - 13

- **Sawyer & Wren Kingston**
    - Knox Kingston - 17
    - Crew Kingston - 14

- **Hudson & Maddie Kingston**
    - Teagan Kingston - 18
    - Aurora Kingston - 15
    - Brooklyn Kingston - 10

- **Amelia & Sam Beneventi**
    - Maddox Beneventi - 23
    - Caitlin Beneventi - 20
    - Roman Beneventi - 18

- Lucky Beneventi - 16

- **Lenny & Bash Beneventi**
  - Maverick Beneventi - 21
  - Ryker Beneventi - 19

- **Jace & India Kingston**
  - Cohen Kingston - 17
  - Saylor Kingston - 12
  - Atlas Kingston - 9
  - Asher Kingston - 9

For family trees, please visit my website
www.authorbellamatthews.com

GRACE

"You know, it's not nice to be prettier than the bride."

I spin around and yelp, as my Christian Louboutin slips in the icy snow beneath my feet.

Oh, come on...

That's not my only thought as the ice-cold, snow-covered ground comes flying up toward my face—just my first—before two giant arms catch me, stopping my fall. "I've got you, tiny dancer."

That voice...

"What the heck, Ares?" My fingers dig into my newly minted brother-in-law's brother's big ass biceps as I cling to him for support while I get my bearings. "You scared the shit out of me. Give a girl a warning next time."

I take a step back, slightly more careful this time, and a shiver skirts down my spine.

Not sure if this one is from the cold or the man.

"Damn, good twin. What crawled up your tutu?" Ares shrugs out of his dark tux jacket and drapes it over my bare shoulders, even though I just cursed him out, solidifying that, in fact, it was the man who caused the shiver.

Damn man.

"Nothing," I lie and slide my arms into the jacket, enjoying the cool, crisp cedar and sandalwood scent that envelops me. Good lord, this man always smells good. "I'm fine. We should go back inside." Leave it to my twin sister to get married during the biggest snowstorm Kroydon Hills has seen in over twenty years. The wedding was already supposed to be small, but the storm cut the original guest list in half, leaving only our closest friends and any family who already live within the city limits. And apparently, each of them is nosier than the last.

"Pretty sure you're not supposed to stand out in a snowstorm in *that* dress, not that I'm complaining." He crosses the lapels of his jacket across my chest and runs his hands up and down my arms. "You might have everyone in there fooled, but I'm not as blind as the rest of them. Your smile's been sad today."

"You've known me for like two months, god of war . . . you don't know my smile." There goes that damn chill again. "And I don't know what you're talking about."

But when I raise my eyes to meet his stormy blue ones, my carefully constructed wall weakens, and that first crack stings like a bitch.

Ares sees it too. His ever-present cocky grin kicks up just a little higher on the right side than the left. I'm not sure I've ever met a man who smiles as much as he does.

"You're infuriating, you know that? You get off acting like an ass, but there's secretly a decent guy under that swagger, isn't there?"

"I've been called worse." He slings an arm around my shoulders and guides me to the glass doors leading back into the dimly lit hotel ballroom. "Come on. Let's get you inside and get a drink in you to warm you up. Then you can spill all your dirty little secrets."

"Who says I have dirty secrets?" I counter, knowing full well he'd run fast and far if he only knew. They all would.

The French doors click shut behind us as the strains of a Lumineers song plays through the sound system. "We all have dirty secrets, Grace. Some are just more fun to figure out than others."

Ares. The god of war. Tall, broad, insanely muscular, and devastatingly dark and handsome. All too perfect for this Greek god.

A moment later, he turns that smile on me and hands me a fancy glass full of Everly and Cross's signature wedding cocktail. I look at it skeptically while Ares taps a bottle of beer against the glass. "Want to tell me what's going on?"

I take a sip, leaving my eyes on his, then choke back a cough and hiss as the liquor burns my throat. "Oh my God. This is awful."

"Yeah. Pretty sure the bartender is the owner's kid or something. I heard a rumor the actual bartender couldn't make it in because of the snow." He grins and lifts his bottle. "That's why I'm sticking to beer."

I take another sip, then set the glass down on the bar and internally debate whether I want to be able to remember tonight when I wake up tomorrow.

If I finish that glass, I may not have the option.

I opt for plan B and snatch Ares's beer from his hand, run my finger over the lip, and take a sip.

"I got offered a job this morning," I answer quietly, unable to believe I said the words out loud.

Completely unfazed, he picks up my glass and throws back half of it in one gulp. "Yeah. That's fucking awful." Then he swallows the rest. "But congrats on the job. Isn't that good news?" Then, as if he's working through what he just said, his eyes scrunch up at the corners. "Wait . . . I thought you already had a job."

"I was offered a better one today." I turn and find us an unoccupied table—easy to do in a room that's supposed to seat two hundred and fifty but has less than fifty people in it. I can feel him behind me before I sit down. Something about this man is magnetic, not that I'll ever admit that to him.

"So what's the problem if it's a better job? Are the tutus ugly or something?" He laughs, and the sound is deep and dark and makes me think forbidden thoughts.

And like the good girl I'm expected to be, I ignore how much I like it and shake my head.

"It's in London . . ." I blurt out and clamp my lips closed to shut myself up. My stomach turns as anxiety tightens its hold on me. "Oh, God. I haven't told anyone that. You can't say anything. Not to anyone, Ares. I can't let Everly find out today."

"Damn, Grace. London . . . *Wow.*" Shadows from the candlelit table dance across his strong jaw, and a flash of *something* crosses his face. For a minute, I think it's disappointment. But as he leans back in his chair and crosses his massive arms over his muscled chest, I realize it's something else. Something . . . more.

Some men look like giants in their hockey pads but are mere mortals when they take them off. Not Ares though. No . . . this god looks just as big off the ice as he does on it.

And damn, it looks good on him.

Dark hair, always a few days past needing to be cut, dark blue eyes full of mischief, a jaw chiseled from stone, and don't even get me started on the muscles . . . His muscles have muscles. I've been around incredibly fit men for years. Dancers *and* athletes. These muscles are different. Capable of doing harm. Honed from years on the ice. These aren't gym muscles there for the sole purpose of looking pretty.

Then there are the hints I've gotten of his tattoos. The kind that make a good girl stupid . . . The kind a girl wants to trace with her tongue . . . The kind that are the perfect cherry on top of the delicious display of arm porn he's giving me right now.

What is it about a man in a white dress shirt, with the sleeves rolled up, and a chunky brown leather watch wrapped around his wrist that makes me, the good twin, think bad, *bad*, thoughts?

One day, I'll see this man shirtless. It'll be at a family barbecue or a beach vacation. Somewhere already hot. And Ares will jump in the lake or the ocean or my parents' damn pool, then all the ice in Kroydon Hills won't be enough to cool me down. The filthy little fantasies I've been having about him for months will be put to shame once I see the real thing. Because there's no way my overactive imagination could possibly do him justice.

"When do you leave?" His voice is unexpectedly strained, and now I want to know why.

"Like I said, I haven't told Everly yet. Today's her day. I don't want to spoil anything . . ."

A storm grows in Ares's dark eyes as they rake over my skin, leaving tiny goosebumps everywhere they touch. "So you tell her tomorrow," he adds slowly.

"It's my dream job," I force out, as much for him to hear as it is a reminder for myself. "I'll be a principal dancer in The Royal Ballet . . . But I have to leave in three days."

"If it's your dream, they'll be happy for you. You've got a great family, Grace."

It's not that I don't know that or that I doubt it.

My family is amazing and supportive.

It's me.

The idea of moving across the world scares me.

It would be the first time I'm alone indefinitely, and I'm not sure I'm strong enough to survive that.

"Three days, huh . . . ?"

I watch my little cousins run by, but Ares reaches over and tugs on a lock of my hair, demanding my attention.

"How am I supposed to shoot my shot if you're on another continent?"

I catch my lip between my teeth and stare across the table before I laugh. This man always finds a way to lighten the mood. "You're not usually the one taking the shots on the ice, unless it's with your fists, god of war."

"I don't see any ice, Grace," he growls low and sexy, and my God . . . the tiny scrap of satin and lace passing for my panties just got soaked.

I take a small sip of his beer and lick my lips. "There's no shot to shoot. My sister married your brother. We're off-limits."

"The fuck we are, ballerina." He raises a brow, challenging me, and grins. Shame he'll never know how that grin affects me.

"Gracie . . ." My youngest brother, Hendrix, stops next to us and extends a drunken hand to me. "Let's show these assholes how to dance."

"Better not let Mom see you like this, Henny."

"Lighten up, good twin, and come dance with me," he demands.

The crazy playlist, which was thrown together earlier when the band bailed because of the snow, switches to an old family-favorite Journey song. I look across the table at Ares, who's gaze hasn't left mine, and smile before placing my hand in Henny's and slipping out of Ares's tux jacket.

"This conversation isn't over, Grace."

"This conversation never started, Ares."

Ares

"Don't go there, man." Maddox Beneventi drops down in the chair across from mine and passes me another beer.

"Go where?" I ask, accepting the bottle but blowing off Beneventi.

"You're staring at the most protected woman in this room, Wilder. And that was before your brother married her sister."

I glance his way from the corner of my eye, not wanting to look away from how Grace laughs as she lets her little brother spin her around the dance floor. "I figured the most protected woman in the room would be *your* sister, Beneventi."

"Point taken." He nods and sips his beer, making it obvious he's watching the same woman I am. "But *that* woman . . ."—he nods toward Grace—"the one who can light up Main Street with her smile . . . that one doesn't have claws. You screw with my sister, and Caitlin will fuck your shit up all by herself long before my brothers, my dad, or I have you dead and buried. You hurt good twin, and God himself couldn't save you."

When the song switches to a catchy Lizzo tune, the girls all scream and run to the center of the dance floor. That group could suck the air out of any room they walk in. Each of them, including my own sister, is gorgeous. And together, they're something to see. But Grace . . . Grace is a fucking knockout. A seductive angel in a soft, pale-purple dress that shows off her delicate curves with long, soft ribbons tied at her neck and hanging loose down her back, tempting a man to tug. It dips down low in the front, clinging to her chest, and cinches in at the waist before it floats out around her hips and legs. And that hair ... Damn, I love her hair. It's long and brown and falling out of the perfect up-do it was in earlier.

I thought everyone was going to shit when she dyed it last month, but it's absolute perfection on her. And man, does it make her aqua eyes sparkle.

She's gorgeous and sweet as hell.

The perfect one-two punch.

And she's leaving in three damn days.

My smile kicks up at the corners when I realize she told me about her job but not Beneventi. Fucker loves to know everything that's going on with his people.

I turn to face him and take another pull of my beer. "You got a thing for Grace, Maddox?"

"Nah ... Told your brother the same thing about Everly. I look at those girls the same way I look at Caitlin. They're family. Just remember, nobody fucks with my family, and we're good, Wilder." He holds my stare, making sure I'm picking up what he's putting down.

"I hear you, man."

And I do hear him.

Doesn't mean I give a shit what he thinks.

This fucker isn't the first person to underestimate me. Won't be the last either. When you grow up in Cross Wilder's shadow, it's hard for people not to underestimate you. And I get it. Cross is *that* guy. The one everything comes easy for. Motherfucker has always been the best hockey player on any rink he's ever put a skate on. He's the fastest. The best shot. Hell, he was even the best in school. Had full-ride offers to go Ivy League before he decided to forgo college and enter the pros right out of high school.

You'd think that would be a shit ton to live up to, but you'd be wrong. Because big brother was so fucking perfect, nobody expected anything from me. They focused all their expectations on him. Made it real easy to fly under the radar. Made it even easier to surprise everyone when I succeeded—because their expectations weren't low, they were nonexistent.

I like when people underestimate me.

It lets me catch them off guard.

They never see me coming.

The music changes, and the song slows to Sam Smith. For a brief moment, I watch something sad flash across Grace's face, and I don't fucking like it.

Without another thought, I push back from the table and tune out whatever Maddox is saying. I have someone more important in my sights. The girls disburse, and I stride past my sister, who's dancing with Maddox's little brother, and almost stop to fuck with him. *Almost.* But I've got better things to do.

I reach Grace as she turns to walk off the dance floor. "Can I have this dance, beautiful?"

Her face flushes a pretty pink, and she closes her eyes for a flash of a second. Then she shakes her head with a soft smile but still places her hand in mine. Everything about this woman is elusive and elegant. And it's plain as day why everyone and their brother wants to protect Grace Sinclair. She's different from anyone I've ever met.

"I've got you, Gracie," I whisper as I pull her against me, and Sam Smith sings about staying.

Fitting.

She gently shakes her head again. "Pretty sure this isn't a good idea."

"Says who?" I wrap an arm around her and press my palm

to the small of her back. She fits perfectly against me, molding to my chest. "We're just dancing."

Grace snakes a hand around my neck, her fingers digging into my hair. "I dance every day, Ares. And it never felt like I was doing something wrong before."

"It's just a dance, Grace." I skim my fingers up and down her spine, enjoying the tremor the action elicits. "I've never danced with a ballerina before."

She lifts her eyes to mine, a torn smile spreading on her lips. "I don't remember a time I didn't want to be a ballerina."

"And now you're going to dance in London." I regret the words the minute they come out of my mouth. Grace's shoulders tighten as she looks away, her eyes catching on Everly and Cross laughing as they dance together.

"Three days never felt so monumental before. I've got tonight and tomorrow night. I'm not sure if I want them to fly by or if I never want them to end."

"Cross and I leave early tomorrow for an away game. You'll have Everly to yourself then."

"That means tonight is my last night before everything changes," she says almost wistfully.

"One night, huh?" I run my hand up the back of her neck and anchor it in her hair. "What are you going to do with it?"

She nibbles her glossy bottom lip, and her aqua eyes shine. "I hadn't thought past the wedding. Why? Do you have any ideas?"

"Yeah. Stay with me."

GRACE

This man and that sexy grin are trouble with a capital T.

I open my mouth to remind him just how off-limits we are, but something makes me stop. Maybe it's the way his stormy blue eyes deepen to nearly black as the smile slides off his face. Or maybe it's the feel of his fingers, powerful and rough, gripping the back of my neck. Hell, maybe it's the sheer fact that I haven't been touched by a man in any way other than dance in so damn long that the idea of spending time with the sexiest man I've ever met, *even if it can't lead to sex*, at the very least means I get more mental material for the next time I'm alone with my vibrator.

Whatever it is, I want more.

I run my teeth over my bottom lip and bite them closed while I watch the most seductive damn grin spread across his face again.

"That's a good girl," he whispers against my skin, and an involuntary shiver pirouettes down my spine. "What do you say we steal a bottle of champagne and a tray of those baby lamb chops and go upstairs to my room?"

I nod, uncertain of anything that came out of his mouth after *good girl*. My goodness . . .

When he says it, it doesn't sound good. It sounds bad in panty-meltingly *good* ways.

I wonder what else I could do to hear that again . . .

Damn it.

Everything about this man goes against every–single–rule that's ever been laid down, and I don't break the rules. No . . . the good twin would never do that.

But maybe . . . just this once . . .

I look up at him, and my breath catches in my chest.

Am I really considering this?

Ares never takes anything seriously.

He's a so-called *bad boy*.

The teammate most likely to fight someone on the ice or off, and now he's my sister's brother-in-law. This is a terrible idea . . . *But* . . . What if it isn't?

Better yet, what if I can't find the strength tonight to care?

I press my palm against his strong chest, thinking I'm going to back away . . . I mean, that's the responsible thing to do. But maybe I'm tired of being responsible. Perfection is an exhausting illusion to maintain. And yet I do so for the sake of everyone else.

Maybe . . . just maybe, I could do this one thing for me.

Sensing my apprehension, Ares covers my hand with his and sighs as he holds me there, locked in a stare-off. "Nothing needs to happen, Grace. We can dance the rest of the night away right here and forget I said anything."

The song ends, rolling into another sultry beat, and I press closer. "What if I don't want to forget?"

"Then I grab that tray of finger food and a bottle of champagne." This time that damn grin is triumphant and electrifying, and I know what I want to do.

"You get the snacks, and I'll steal us some cake. What's your room number?" I force the words out quickly as my eyes dart around us, and my heart thunders behind my ribs like the ultimate crescendo in my favorite ballet.

Ares steps back and pulls two key cards from his pocket. He presses one in my hand and palms the other. "Room 626, Grace."

The key card weighs heavy in my hand as I nod, and Ares backs away.

I watch as he pockets two magnums of champagne and grabs a tray of finger food without anyone blinking an eye. I don't think anyone at all paid him a bit of attention. How is that possible? The eyes of the world are constantly on me. Maybe *the world* is a bit of an exaggeration, but it certainly feels that way most days. I can't do anything at all without being seen and fretted over.

Getting out of here unnoticed ought to be interesting.

Quickly, I dart across the massive ballroom and grab my purse from the table, but before I can take another step, Dad's voice stops me.

"Hey, Gracie. Come dance with your old man."

I hesitate, feeling what has to be a metric ton of guilt swimming in my eyes, then force a perfect smile. "Of course, Daddy."

"Do you remember when you would stand on my feet and beg me to dance you around the living room?" His voice is hoarse and wistful, like he's lost in a memory. One I can visualize with scary clarity.

"Of course I do," I tell him right before he spins me out, then back in again. "You'll always be my favorite dance partner."

"Don't make promises you can't keep, Gracie girl. One day, some lucky man, who could never possibly be good enough, is going to sweep you off your feet, and you're going to leave me just like your sister did."

Or maybe I'm going to break his heart and leave him this week...

I rest my head on his shoulder and close my eyes. "You didn't lose her, Dad. She lives five minutes from your house and works three buildings down from Mom. She's right here, and she just gave you two grandbabies to dote on too."

Dad chuckles and presses a kiss to my head. "You always find a way to spin everything for the better, Gracie."

And there's another inadvertent hit.

I'm going to break his heart.

I know it.

What I want to say is *please don't hate me when I move across the world to follow my dreams, Daddy.* But I know that's not Declan Sinclair's way. *No.* My dad has always been my biggest cheerleader. He's encouraged me to follow every dream and never once made me feel bad about how far away or how long they'd take me away.

"Love you, Gracie." He kisses the top of my head, and my first tear silently falls.

I choke back the sob threatening to bubble up. "Love you too, Dad."

*I*t takes me nearly twenty-five minutes to successfully navigate my family, a handful of friends, and my new niece, Kerrigan—who wanted to show me how her dress twirls when she spins—and manage to snag two pieces of cake and two forks without any questions. Okay, so Ares did it in five, but I'll settle for my time. At least

I didn't chicken out. I've thankfully *successfully* slipped on and off the elevator without anyone blinking an eye. No small feat for some, but I consider it a major accomplishment for me.

That is, until I stop in front of Ares's door and realize the key he gave me is in my purse. The sparkly silver one I'm holding under my arm. *Okay, Grace, you've got this.* I attempt to maneuver the plates and forks into one hand so I can get the key, but a piece of chocolate cake pays the ultimate price. The plate shatters and the cake paints the door, the wall, and my shoes with chocolate.

Damn it. I really liked these shoes.

The door opens, and I look up to find Ares standing there, chuckling, and oh my . . . he looks more delicious than the dearly departed cake. "You look like you're considering eating that cake off the floor, good twin."

"More like lamenting the loss rather than considering my options." Proud that I managed to answer at all, I move around him into the room and put the sole-surviving cake and my purse down carefully on the bedside table, right next to his pilfered goods.

The Kroydon Hills Plaza is a recently restored beauty from the 1920s. The rooms are small but beautiful. One king-sized bed takes up most of the limited space, similar to my own room a floor below. A big window overlooks the woods surrounding the center of town, framing the space and showcasing the snow glowing silver in the moonlight as it falls in big fat flakes covering the world below.

An overnight bag is open with clothes spilling out, strewn on the only chair in the room, and no big shock, a hockey game is playing on a muted TV.

Ares closes the door behind himself and hurries over to the chair to toss the bag into the closet. "Sorry," he mumbles, and I immediately decide I like this side of him. The shoes kicked off, sleeves rolled up, messy side. Far from perfect. Not putting on any kind of show for anyone and looking so damn attractive without any effort at all.

He eyes the food, then me. "So . . . I guess I'm supposed to let you have the cake, right?"

I have no control over the ridiculous laughter that bubbles out of me. It's not even that funny, but I laugh so long and so loud, my ribs hurt. I laugh so obnoxiously that when I finally stop, Ares is looking at me like I should have two heads, and that makes me laugh again.

"You okay there, Grace?"

I shake my head, kick off my heels, yank up my dress in an incredibly ungraceful way, grab the cake, and then drop down on the bed. "Do you know my favorite thing about you?"

The poor guy looks at me like it's a trap. "You have a favorite thing about me?"

"I'm serious, god of war." I break off a piece of cake with the side of the fork and offer it to him, then happily watch as his lips wrap around the tines of the silverware. "You treat me differently than everyone else. You don't act like I'm made of glass."

"Are you gonna shatter?" he asks, and I shake my head. "I think they all underestimate you, good twin. I know a thing about that."

Scary how right he is. Then, as if I've become someone completely unknown to me, I reach up with my thumb and wipe away chocolate cake crumbs from his full lips. Ares's eyes darken to a nearly navy blue, and oh my . . . I like that look on him. "They do think I'm fragile. They always have."

"What do you think, Grace?"

When I don't answer him, he doesn't push . . . No, instead he picks up one of the two bottles of procured champagne with a wicked look in those stormy eyes. "Let's see if I can get this." The cork pops and shoots across the room, and a spray of champagne follows until two coffee mugs are filled. Ares hands me one. "Do you like champagne?"

I sip from the coffee cup and smile. "I do tonight."

Okay, who is this flirty girl? And where the hell did she come from? Because she sure as shit doesn't seem like me.

"I'm usually more of a beer guy, but this isn't bad," he agrees and grabs the plate full of appetizers as he moves next to me on the bed. "Hungry?"

I nibble my bottom lip and try to remember the last thing I ate. "I may have forgotten to eat today."

"How does someone forget to eat?" Ares sits down next to me, close enough to touch but not quite touching, and leans back against the gray upholstered headboard. He grabs the tray from the table and holds out a mini quiche in offering.

I decline and sip from my coffee mug as I watch Ares pop it in his mouth instead.

Can the act of swallowing be hot?

My cheeks flush when I realize it would be if I was doing the swallowing.

Then I wonder where this dirty mind is coming from.

"So tell me what it's like to dance . . ."

"That's a really open question, Wilder." I run my fork through the chocolate-raspberry cream sandwiched between the layers of death by chocolate sponge cake, then close my eyes and savor the sweet taste on my tongue before I answer him. "It's amazing and terrifying wrapped up in one perfectly pink silk ribbon. All the work. The years of training. The torture we put our bodies through . . . as well as our minds. You sell your soul for this once in a lifetime chance at perfection, but it's ballet. No one is ever good enough." I sigh and look over at the snow falling. It's easy to see the beauty in it, and that's kind of like ballet. Beautiful and treacherous.

"But if the stars align in your favor . . . If you've worked harder. Trained longer. And trusted your muscles enough to remember, even when your mind blanks and everything else around you ceases to exist . . . if you're that one in a million whose dreams become reality. It's magic."

I close my eyes and inhale, straightening my spine and sitting taller on the bed, as things come into focus. The chill of the air on the exposed skin of my arms. The chiffon ribbon trailing down my bare back. The sandalwood and cedar scent of the delicious man next to me. The warmth emanating from his skin. Skin that isn't even touching my own.

And when I open my eyes, he's watching with fascination. "For two hours a night, you get to perform on that stage, and there's no bigger, better high you could ever possibly get than that."

For once, he doesn't smile.

He doesn't speak.

I'd almost dare to say he doesn't breathe as his hand reaches for my face, invading my personal space with a calloused thumb that skims my cheek.

"Are you sure you have to leave in three days, Grace?"

My eyes caress every strong line of his face. "My official offer is waiting in my email."

He nods in slow motion before he drops his hand and takes my hopes with him. Then Ares raises his coffee cup and taps it to the one sitting in my lap. "I can't wait to see you dance one day . . ."

ARES

*G*race and I finished a bottle and a half of champagne, all the appetizers, and the single piece of chocolate cake while we spent the night talking. *Never did that before.* Just talked.

Not that I didn't want to do more—because I did.

A fuck of a lot more.

But it didn't feel right.

Not with her.

With her, everything just feels... *more.*

We've both been quiet for a while when I reach over and shut off the light, leaving us bathed in the silvery moonlight.

Grace rests her head on my shoulder with a sweet sigh. "What time do you have to leave tomorrow?"

I run my hand through her hair, wishing like hell things were different. "I've got a few hours." She looks so peaceful next to me as she closes her eyes and her lashes fan her cheeks, but there's no way she can be comfortable in that dress. I unbutton my dress shirt and hand it to her. "Here. Put this on. It's got to be more comfortable than that dress."

Her heavy eyes look from the shirt to me before she

stands and does some kind of fancy voodoo shit where she puts the button-down on, then manages to slip out of the dress without ever showing me an extra sliver of skin. "Damn. That was impressive."

"Quick changes are a ballerina's specialty," she tells me just before she yawns and tucks herself under the blanket. "Lie down with me, Ares."

Her voice is quiet and hesitant. She's nervous . . . needlessly so, because I'm not sure I'll ever be able to deny her anything.

Grace Sinclair has managed to grab hold of me like no one else ever has, without ever lifting one of her delicate fingers.

I kick off my pants, leave on my boxers, get back in next to her, then wrap an arm around her beautiful body while I try to keep my own under control.

Grace rests her head on my chest and yawns again. "I knew you'd have a beautiful chest, god of war."

A laugh rumbles through me. "Pretty sure you've had too much champagne, beautiful."

"Maybe . . ." She traces my tattoo with the tip of her finger, lighting every nerve on fire as her eyes grow heavier. "Why couldn't we have met a year ago, Ares?"

"We weren't ready then, tiny dancer," I tell her and shake my head as realization dawns.

She's already fallen asleep.

I'm not sure I've ever spent an entire night in bed, just talking with a woman, but I could have listened to her for days. The way her whole face lights up when she mentions her family, her fierce loyalty to her friends and this town . . . and the love-hate relationship she has with ballet. All of it. I hung on every damn word, like a puppy ready to beg for any scraps of her attention I could get. And even now, with her asleep in my arms and absolutely no chance of anything happening tonight, I'm not sure I'd have changed a minute of it.

Somewhere in the depths of my mind, someone calls my name.

It doesn't sound human.

Just a sound I hear but ignore.

I've got a beautiful woman, soft and pliant and asleep in my arms, and I'm not ready to let her go just yet. Not when I'm going to spend the next two days with the team while she flies across the world.

"Ares," Grace murmurs against my chest before her grip around my waist tightens. Her long, smooth legs are tangled with mine, and all her soft curves are fitted against me as if she were made for me. "Ares..."

I almost press my lips against the top of her head but stop before I can and inhale her citrusy-vanilla scent instead.

She's not mine to kiss. *Not yet...*

Instead, I relax into the stolen moment.

At least until I hear the damn knock again. "Dude." Fuck me, that pissed-off voice belongs to Easton Hayes, my teammate and Grace's best friend's husband.

Shit. I look around for the time, but don't see a clock anywhere before Grace sits up and rubs her eyes.

I cup her face in my hands. "Don't move."

Her sleepy eyes blink up at me, and she yawns, looking utterly fuckable.

Noted—this girl doesn't function on no sleep.

I cross the room and crack open the door, then move so

I'm blocking any view Hayes may have of my bed. "What the hell, man?"

Easton's brows raise in question. "Late night, Wilder?"

When I don't answer, he crosses his arms over his chest and grins.

Cocky fucker.

"Got some company in there?"

Yeah. Still not answering.

"Well, tell them you're on a schedule here. You've got to be downstairs in an hour so we can meet the team plane. We're all heading down for breakfast now."

I run my hand through my hair and grip the door. "I'm good, man. My bag and Cross's are both in the truck already. I'll be down soon."

"Hope she was worth it." The stupid fucking grin on his face grows right along with my urge to knock it right off his smug face. "One hour, Ares. Don't make the team wait over a piece of ass."

"Fuck off, Easton." Anger burns just under my skin as my grip on the damn door threatens to splinter the wood beneath my fingers.

I shut the fucking thing slowly, knowing Grace heard every word.

When I turn, I find her standing next to the bed in my dress shirt. Her long, toned legs are bare and beautiful and would look so fucking good wrapped around my face. *Damn* . . .

Grace's arms are wrapped tightly over her chest as if she's protecting herself. And I hope like hell I'm not who she thinks she needs protecting from.

"Wow." She fidgets from foot to foot. "I feel like I need to do the walk of shame, and we didn't even have sex."

Well, now I feel like a piece of fucking shit. "Ignore him, Grace. He thinks you're—"

"Like every other woman he's probably known was in one of your many, *many* hotel rooms. It's okay, Ares. I know what this is."

I cross the room in two long strides, fucking annoyed that she'd ever think she wasn't more than anyone else. "You don't know a damn thing if you think you're anything like any other woman, Grace." I cup her face in my hands, and she sucks in a quiet breath. "You are so much more."

Her lids close, and long black lashes flutter against her pale-pink cheeks. "Last night," she whispers, then opens her eyes and swallows. "I had a really nice night, Ares."

There's no misunderstanding the brush-off she's about to give me, so I run my thumb over her pouty bottom lip and counter before she can. "Last night was one of the best nights I've had in years, Grace."

"Then why didn't you kiss me?" Her words are whispered but pack a powerful punch. One I wasn't expecting. So, I do what I do best and answer with brutal honesty.

"Because when I kiss you, it's going to be the start of something great, Grace. And you're not ready for that. You're leaving. You haven't talked to your family about it. And it's obvious you're already torn. I'm not going to be a factor in your decision. I can't be your excuse. Go do this thing. Be great, and I'll be here when you come back."

She runs her teeth over her bottom lip, and tears pool in her sparkling eyes. "You can't promise that. I don't know when I'm coming home." Gracie wipes at her cheeks and lifts her chin. "I don't even know *if* I'm coming home . . . My God. I'm not even sure if I'm going."

"You're going, and you're going to be amazing, Grace. And when you're ready, we're going to be everything." I wrap my arms around her soft body and hold her tight for a minute, wondering when I turned into this guy. The one who cares enough to urge someone to follow their dreams instead of selfishly pushing for what I want. Because right now, I want this woman in my arms more than I've wanted anything in a long fucking time. But my gut is screaming she's worth the wait.

Something tells me Grace Sinclair is special in a way no other woman will ever be.

But the timing isn't right. *Not yet.*

"How can you be so sure?" she asks sweetly.

"I just am." I run my hand over her soft hair. "You're going to have to trust me."

Grace rests her head against my chest and sniffles. "I kinda thought you were a manwhore, god of war."

"It's easier to let everyone think that than to correct them all the time, good twin." I smile as she tugs away from me.

"I know that feeling." She lifts up on her toes and kisses my cheek. "Thank you for being a gentleman last night. Any chance you've got something I could wear to make the walk of shame to my room slightly less obvious? I mean I can put my dress back on—"

"I got you." I step back and reach into my bag and pull out sweats and a hoodie. "You're going to swim in these, and they're not some fancy name brand, but they'll be more comfortable than that dress." I hand them to her, and her smile lights up the room like only Grace Sinclair's can. "In case I didn't say it, you looked really pretty in that dress, Grace."

Her cheeks flush pink, and she holds the clothes against her chest as she walks into the bathroom. "I would have looked even better out of it, Ares."

I throw my head up to the ceiling and close my eyes, wondering what the hell I just did.

GRACE

    I wait about fifteen minutes after Ares leaves to creep out of his hotel room in hopes that everyone else is already downstairs at the breakfast my parents are hosting. My pulse races, and my palms sweat like I'm about to set foot on a grand stage in front of the largest audience of my career, when in reality, I'm hoping not one single soul sees me before I get to my room.

As the elevator doors begin to close, I let out a sigh of relief, until a dainty hand with a bracelet I'd know anywhere pushes the doors open.

Shit.

"Oh, thank God. Your sister has been blowing up my phone for ten minutes already." Brynlee rushes in with a huff, relieved she made it at first, then tilts her head to the side, squints her eyes, and purses her perfectly glossed lips. "Gracie . . . Ummm . . ." The words are slow and kinda quiet as her eyes scan over me from head to toe. And before I know what's happening, her eyes grow as big as dinner plates, and a noise I'm not quite sure anyone other than dogs could actually hear squeals past her lips. "Ohmyfuckinggod, Grace Sinclair. That's Ares Wilder's hoodie. It's got his number on the fucking sleeve. And. You're. Wearing. It."

I press my hand against her mouth and glare at my best friend. "Shut up, Brynnie. Seriously." The elevator chimes, and the doors slide open on my floor. Carefully, as if I'm about to steal a Monet off the wall of the Louvre, I peek out to make sure there aren't any other witnesses.

Okay... The coast is clear.

With a tight grip, I pull Brynlee behind me out of the elevator and down the hall to my room. Then I shove both of us safely inside so no one else can see what I'm wearing.

Maybe I should have just stuck with the dress.

Fuck a duck.

I breathe out a sigh of relief once the door clicks shut behind us and drop my shoes and dress down on the chair. I could use a nap, a shower, and some ibuprofen. Maybe not in that order.

"Grace," Brynn screeches. "Everly is waiting for me downstairs. What the hell are we doing?"

I close my eyes and massage my temples.

Stupid champagne.

When I open my eyes, she's staring at me, waiting. "I'm shutting you up and throwing on my own damn clothes, Brynn. What's it look like I'm doing?"

She drops down onto my very un-slept-in bed and crosses her legs primly. "It looks like you're doing the walk of shame from Ares Wilder's room, if you really want to know. Now get your perfect ass changed, good twin, and tell me he fucks like the god he is—because that man has a body chiseled out of stone, and I'd know. I've had my hands all over him on my table. He's a work of art. And he's even cockier than Cross. I mean, come on... it's got to be at least nine inches, right?"

I stand there for a moment, shocked stupid. "Brynlee . . . What the . . . I mean . . ." Words absolutely fail me. "You're their physical therapist," I sputter, and the bitch laughs. Well . . . more like cackles.

"I am." She pulls a Chapstick from her purse, coats her lips, then pops them together and smiles. "But I'm a woman, and these men are elite athletes with bodies honed from years spent on skates. I may be a professional, but I'm not blind, Gracie. A girl can appreciate eye candy, can't she?"

I grab my clothes from my overnight bag and walk into the bathroom to brush my teeth and change but leave the door open to finish our conversation. "Well, sorry to disappoint," I tell her as I search through my toiletries case for . . . *Where the hell is the toothpaste?* "We didn't have sex."

"What?" she screeches.

Found it.

Now where's the damn toothbrush?

"We talked. I drank too much champagne and stayed in his room instead of bothering to come down here."

"Then why were you in his sweats, Grace Elizabeth Sinclair?"

I spit out the toothpaste and groan. "Why am I getting full-named?"

"Because you're wearing Ares Wilder's clothes. *Ares*. The god of war. You had your first one-night stand with Ares Wilder," she yells, and I want to kill her. "I'm so proud of you."

"I. Did. Not. Fuck. Ares." I step out of the clothes in question and into my own, and I may or may not miss the smell of him instantly. *Damn it*. I poke my head back through the doorway. "We slept, Brynnie. Sorry to disappoint you. But that's all that happened. There has to be sex for it to be a one-night stand."

I look in the mirror and flinch.

Not good.

Where's a brush when I need one?

I run my fingers through my dark hair, throw it up in a ponytail, and splash some water on my face. This is as good as it's getting this morning.

When I walk back into my room, Brynn is sitting primly as she stares at me, clearly disappointed by the lack of sex fact. Same, girl. *Same.* "Really? Nothing? Did he at least get you off?"

I shake my head. "It wasn't like that."

"What a waste of a perfectly good manwhore."

My stomach sours at her words. "Don't say that, please." I grab my portable phone charger and toss it in my purse with my dead phone, then snag my sneakers and slide them on. "I may need your help today."

"Name it," she says without hesitation because that's what we've always done for each other. The five of us have always, *always* looked out for each other ever since we were little girls. "I'm going to miss you so much, Brynnie." I sniff.

"What the hell, Grace?" She stands up and waits as I tie my shoe.

"I got offered a place as a principal dancer with The Royal Ballet . . . in London." I wait and watch as my words sink in, and a tiny bit of my trepidation fades when her face transforms into pure excitement.

"Oh my God, Grace," she screams as she reaches for me, jumping up and down. "This is your dream. You're doing it. You're living it. You're going to dance in London." Her fingers dig in where she's gripping my biceps now that we're both jumping like little kids until she yanks us both to an abrupt stop. A myriad of emotions flash across her face before she settles on a look I know too damn well.

"When do you leave?"

I stare into her bright, beautiful, green eyes and rip that

Band-Aid off in a flash, scared if I don't do it now, I won't do it at all. "In two days."

"And when are we telling Evie?"

"Can I tell you how much I love that you said *we*?" I pull her in for a hug, and her phone rings obnoxiously from the bed.

"I don't even have to look to know that's Evie. We've got to get down to breakfast, now, good twin."

"Do we have to?" This is so not going to end well.

Brynlee and I stroll into the restaurant on the first floor of the hotel a few minutes later, and I'm instantly relieved. Everyone is chatting in their own world, and no one gives Brynn and me a second thought.

I slide into an open seat at the far end of one table, across from my brother Nixon, and Brynn sits down next to me.

Call me a chicken, but I'm not ready to face my twin yet.

"Hey, good twin. Nice of you to join us." Nixon grins a stupid fucking grin, and I kick him as hard as I can under the table. Everly and I may be the twins in our family . . . well, in our immediate family—our big ass family has a few sets. *Anyway . . . I digress*. We may be the twins, but Nix is barely a year younger than us. The three of us, Maddox, and Callen all grew up kinda like a box set. Where one went and what one did, we all went, and we all did. This little shit knows something. Or at the very least, he thinks he does.

Maddox drops down in the seat next to Nixon and hands him a Bloody Mary that looks more like a full-blown brunch than it does a drink. A skewer stacked thick with plump, oversized shrimp, crispy bacon, and enough veggies to count as a small salad poke out, and my stomach turns a little.

Definitely too much champagne last night.

Heat warms my cheeks as the memory of us opening the second bottle surfaces.

The way we laughed as the cork flew across the room and

the way Ares sucked the spilled liquid off his thumb. Fuck, I wanted to be that thumb.

Nixon stares at me for a beat too long, seeing a little too much, then laughs. "Damn, good twin. Good for you."

"Drink your breakfast, Nix," Brynlee chastises him, pulling the attention from me, thankfully.

Kenzie reaches around Maddox and steals Nix's drink. "Don't be a douche, Nix."

I love my friends.

"Fuck, man. You're screwed when they're ganging up on you." Maddox protects his drink, like it's his precious and he's Gollum in a cave. "You busting your sister's balls about where she slept or about the new job?"

My eyes fly to him as my entire body recoils from the one-two punch. "What the fuck, Madman?"

"You need to work on your situational awareness at family functions, good twin." His words are more callous than I'm used to coming from him, and I instantly realize it's retaliation. He's hurt. Damn it.

And like an accident you see happening in slow motion but are helpless to stop, Everly has just walked over. "What new job?" She looks between Brynn and me with a mimosa in her hand.

Brynn takes Everly's drink. "It's not me."

My twin sister's gaze falls on me. "I didn't know you were looking for a new company. Is it the Philadelphia Ballet?"

When I meet her eyes, she knows immediately, even if she doesn't want to admit it. "New York?" she asks, and I shake my head. "Shit, Gracie. Are you going to San Francisco? You can't seriously be considering moving across the country."

She's listing all the companies we used to dream about dancing for when we were little.

All but the one that was our ultimate goal.

"What?" Mom asks from the other end of the table.

Apparently, superhuman parental hearing doesn't go away as your kids get older.

I swear to God, I'm going to kill Maddox with my bare hands for this.

"Gracie's moving to San Francisco," Hendrix, who I hadn't even noticed before now, tells her right before Leo smacks his head. Middle brother to the rescue.

"She didn't say that," Leo argues.

"She didn't say it wasn't that either though," Nixon corrects Leo.

And I'm going to bury my brothers right along with Maddox.

An ocean between us is looking like a good thing right about now.

"Stop." I push back and stand up from my chair, nearly knocking it over in the process. I take Everly's hand in mine and squeeze. "I'm so sorry. I didn't want to talk about this now. I didn't want to ruin your weekend."

"Grace." She looks at me with hurt already swimming in her eyes. "What aren't you saying?"

My stomach bottoms out, leaving me with an awful feeling.

I hate doing this. I don't disappoint people. It's not in my DNA.

And this is worse because this won't just be disappointment.

This is going to hurt my twin sister.

How many people can I hurt in one morning?

I look at my mirror image and link our pinkies. "I was offered a principal position with The Royal Ballet in London."

A million emotions fly over Everly's face before she finally manages one single word. "When?"

"In two days . . . if I go." I ignore the chaos erupting around me and whisper, "I'm so sorry, sissy."

Tears flood her eyes, and she pulls me in for a hug. "You're going."

GRACE

EVERLY

Text when you land, okay?

KENZIE

I hope you found a hot Brit with a sexy accent on the plane and joined the mile-high club. I always wanted to join that club.

BRYNLEE

You were in every other club in school. I'm surprised there are any left you didn't make your bitch, Kenz.

LINDY

Overachiever much?

KENZIE

Says the gold medalist . . .

LINDY

Point taken.

KENZIE

Mile-high club. Make it your mission, Gracie.

EVERLY

Text us so many pictures it feels like we're there with you, sissy.

KENZIE

Again – focus on the hot British men, Grace. I wouldn't complain if you sent tons of pics of hot men.

LINDY

What the hell, Kenz?

KENZIE

I'm in my final semester of med school. I haven't had a date since tenth grade. AND my vibrator died a slow, sad, painful death before I was done with it last night. Do you think Amazon offers same day deliveries?

EVERLY

For vibrators?

BRYNLEE

They do. But you have to search personal massage tools.

LINDY

And you know this how, Brynnie?

BRYNLEE

We don't all have super sexy husbands to give us multiple orgasms, Lindy!

KENZIE

I just threw up in my mouth, Brynnie. That's my brother you're talking about.

BRYNLEE

I know. I just block out that it's Easton when Lindy talks about the sex.

KENZIE

She. Does. Not. Talk. About. Sex. With. My. Brother.

LINDY

Not with you, I don't. But I'm pretty sure we kept Maddox up all night after the wedding. Those walls were thin. And he yelled back at one point.

KENZIE

You suck so fucking bad.

LINDY

Easton likes the way I suck. Thank you very much.

KENZIE

I hate you.

EVERLY

You love us.

BRYNLEE

Pics, Gracie. We want to see everything.

I choke back my laugh after the flight attendant tells us we can turn airplane mode off, and I read through my friend's messages.

GRACE

No mile-high club this time. I sat next to a very kind older gentleman who spent the entire flight talking about Winston Churchill and what he did for Britain. I think he kept talking after I put my earbuds in and eye mask on because he was still talking when we landed. I've gotta give him credit. The man had stamina.

> I'm off to find the apartment and roommate the company helped place me with and have my first practice tomorrow. I'll send pics soon. XOXO

Six weeks later

"They're all going to be clamoring for you now, Grace." My roommate, Lennon, drops her ballet bag on her bed and walks right to the fridge in our tiny little flat that might just be older than the state I grew up in. One of the things I learned quickly after moving to London was how steeped in history so much of this city is. It makes our country look like a newborn in comparison, and I was instantly smitten with the entire city.

Luckily for me, Lennon is somewhat of a local and was looking for a roommate when I joined the company. She's a few years younger than me and a few inches shorter, but what she lacks in height, she makes up for in spunk. She's also always strangely hyper. Like a little sprite.

"Here." She tosses me a bottle of vitamin water from the fridge. "Drink up. We're meeting at the Drunken Duck in thirty minutes. I call first dibs on the shower."

I'm not sure she actually took a breath while she was speaking.

"Sounds good." I barely get the words out before the bathroom door shuts behind her.

So much energy.

I sit down on my bed and check my phone. I promised I'd send everyone pics tonight. Mom and Dad are flying out to see the show next week, and Everly is trying to come soon, but with the Revolution making the playoffs, her schedule is tight.

A notification I'm not expecting waits for me on my lock screen.

Ares Wilder.

I've never slid my finger across a screen so quickly before.

ARES

You were beautiful tonight, tiny dancer.

What the hell?

GRACE

How would you know, god of war?

ARES

I have my ways.

GRACE

You can't be in London. You have a game in Philly tomorrow.

ARES

Got my scheduled memorized?

GRACE

No. I talked to my sister this morning. She mentioned it.

He doesn't need to know I watch all his games whenever I can.

> ARES
>
> No. I'm not in London. But I'll come see it as soon as the season's over.

> GRACE
>
> Then how do you know how the show was? Come on . . . fess up.

> ARES
>
> What's the use of having pro hockey money if I can't pay someone on the other side of the world to tape something for me?

It takes a minute for his words to sink in . . . and then . . . *What?*

> GRACE
>
> Are you serious?

> ARES
>
> About you? Always.

> GRACE
>
> I'm not sure if that's incredibly sweet or incredibly stalkery.

> ARES
>
> Okay well, let's not go telling anyone I'm sweet, okay? I do have a reputation to maintain.

> GRACE
>
> Right. Wouldn't want anything to crack that manwhore image.

> ARES
>
> Let them think what they want to think.

GRACE
I heard a rumor you were getting your own place.

ARES
Yeah. I'm taking over Lindy and Easton's place now that they bought a house. I can only stand listening to your sister and my brother going at it so many times before I go blind.

GRACE
I don't think it works that way.

ARES
She was on the counter, and he was on his knees, Gracie. Trust me. I don't need to see this shit. I move in this weekend.

GRACE
What about Bellamy?

ARES
She and Caitlyn are looking for a place.

GRACE
With Cait's dad, they better find a fortress because he's not letting her move into anything less.

ARES
Shit. Gotta go, Grace.

GRACE
Bye.

Is it possible for your heart to feel both heavier and somehow lighter at the same time?

GRACE

Never settle for bad coffee, boring friends, or sensible men.
All three should set your soul on fire.
–Grace's secret thoughts

"I don't understand how you can watch this nonsense," Lennon groans as she sits on the floor in front of the sofa I'm lying on and breaks in a new pair of pointe shoes. "You've been here six months now, Grace. Come on..."

"Listen." I toss a piece of air-popped popcorn at her face, then quickly turn back to my MacBook in time to catch Cross taking the puck down the ice. "I've given in and stopped calling soccer *soccer*. The least you can do is stop calling hockey *nonsense*."

I've been trying to catch the Revolution games whenever I can.

Most of the time, I resort to YouTube because different time zones are a bitch.

At least I can still catch them, even if the game was already played twelve hours ago. I put an embargo on the girls. They know not to text me what happens until I tell them I saw the game. Which happens to be killing Evie today. I woke up to three texts asking if I saw it last night, which could be good or bad. The Revolution are fighting for the Stanley Cup. If they won last night, they won the whole thing. If they lost, they've got to finish out the series.

"Just because you don't use the term *soccer* doesn't mean you're using the term *football* correctly, little miss America," she snaps back sarcastically and bangs the hell out of her shoe against the hardwood floor.

We break our shoes so we can build them back the way we want them.

Some dancers burn them with a lighter.

Some scrape their soles with a grater.

I rip out the inside sole.

We all do something to make them bend to our needs and our will.

Ballet is a constant battle.

We bend our shoes, our bodies, and our souls all in the name of the performance.

I move the ice pack on my foot, ignoring the sharp pain shooting into my toes as my director's words from earlier play over and over and over again in my mind.

I'd hate for Tasha to have to dance your part tonight, Miss Sinclair.

Me too, Jenkins. Me too.

"Did you fall asleep on me, Grace?" Lennon bangs with a little extra oomph, bringing me out of my spiraling thoughts.

What had she said . . . ?

I think about it for a second, then remember . . . Right.

Football and soccer. Our age-old fight. "Agree to disagree," I offer because it's the closest we'll ever come to an understanding on our love of sports.

I'm sorry, but to me, football will always be the game my father dominated for over twenty years. And no one, not even my barely twenty-year-old, beautiful ballerina roommate, no matter how quintessentially British she is, is going to change my mind.

"That one is your brother-in-law, right?" She nods toward the screen as Cross gets checked against the boards and Ares comes flying behind the net to take down the player who cross-checked Cross.

"And that one is your secret lov-ah . . ." she teases as my stomach drops.

"He is not."

"Then how come you blush like you're seeing your first knob every time you text him?"

I'll never get used to British slang. There's just something about *knob*. Not like peen or dick are much better, but really . . . *knob*?

"I do not blush. I smile. And I'll have you know I smile whenever I get texts from back home." I wiggle my toes. Yup. Still pain. This ice pack and I have been good friends all week. The throbbing eventually subsides, but each day it seems to last just a little longer.

Pain is an occupational hazard.

It's a daily occurrence.

When you dance at this level, you need a higher pain tolerance than most people could ever hope to have. If you can dance through the pain, you beat it. *You win.* And I refuse to lose.

Lennon reaches into her ballet bag and grabs something, then holds her hand out to me. "You can lie to yourself if that makes you feel better, but you do blush when you talk to him. I mean, come on. I've seen what that man looks like. I'd blush too." She opens her hand and offers me the small tin in her palm. "Here. Take one of these. It'll help."

"What are they?" I take the tin and eye the tiny pills. I've never had to take anything stronger than Advil or ibuprofen before. But this sprain has been killing me for days. And we've got a show tonight.

"They're from a prescription I got last fall. You need to rest that foot for the show. This will help." She says it so nonchalantly. No big deal. *Here, take one.* But she's right. I need to be at my best tonight, and I'm so far from it this week, I'm surprised they haven't threatened to cut me.

I toss it to the back of my throat, sip my water, and watch the last twenty minutes of the game. Then, as the last three seconds of the clock tick down, Ares gets the puck on a breakaway.

Go. *Go.* GO!

He takes it down the ice, skates behind the net to get away from the Vipers' defender, then quickly scoops it right into the net.

Oh. My. God.

He just scored.

Holy shit.

The Revolution just won. *They won the Cup*! Oh . . . My . . . Ahhh . . .

They won.

I grab my phone and squeal. "They. Won!"

"Right," Lennon looks over at my laptop, then back at me as she gets up. "And you don't have a thing for him. Like I said, go ahead and keep lying to yourself." She gathers her bag and pointe shoes and disappears quietly into her bedroom.

I'm not anywhere near ready to unpack that statement.

Ares and I text almost weekly. Sometimes they're flirty.

Sometimes it's just, *hey, good game.* But no matter how short or long the conversation, they make me smile.

> GRACE
>
> OMG. You scored the winning goal. AND WON THE CUP! So excited for you!! I've avoided all social media for the last twelve hours so I could see it for myself, and you won!

I close my text app and scroll social media to see what everyone is saying back home. Sometimes, he texts back right away. Sometimes, it's hours later. Our time difference makes it hard to connect with anyone back home at decent times, and I can only imagine the partying they must have done last night.

It looks like everyone posted pictures.

Everly. Easton and Lindy. Brynlee. My friends and family at the game.

My brothers are there with my cousins and losing their minds.

A heavy sense of homesickness hits me hard.

I'm missing everything.

I wish I was there.

Most days, I can push the ache away. But this . . . this was huge. For Everly and Cross. For Easton and Lindy. For Brynlee. For Ares . . .

I blow up a picture of all my friends and family together, celebrating at West End, the bar in Kroydon Hills that Maddox owns. Cross is kissing the top of Everly's head. Lindy's hanging on Easton. My cousin Callen has a girl on each side. And, oh gross . . . Nixon has a girl in his lap, who looks like she's trying to swallow his tonsils. When I swipe to see the next one, my heart drops. There, in the back corner of the shot, Ares stands behind Nixon, and there's a beautiful girl in his arms.

Ooohh . . . *Yikes.* That hurts a little more than it should.

I mean, it's not like we made any promises, and it has been six months.

Six months of texts, and calls, and FaceTimes.

Half a year of trusting this man with my secrets.

But still . . . I kinda want to rip her nasty hair out of her head and use it to yank her away from him, but I'll just keep that to myself.

As Brynlee would say, *obviously, I woke up and chose violence today.*

But it's more than that. I guess I'm a little hurt too, which I have no business feeling.

My MacBook chimes with an incoming FaceTime, and I wipe a stupid, errant tear from my cheek and sit up straighter before I answer.

Ares's handsome face fills my screen and takes my breath away. He's fresh from a shower with wet hair that's a little longer than he usually keeps it, dripping down and catching on long black lashes framing those dark blue eyes that hold me hostage. They're a little red and tired today, but no less hypnotic.

"Hey." I swallow down any lingering sting and pull my big-girl panties up. *Don't be a baby, Gracie.* "It's the man of the hour. How does it feel to score the game-winning goal, Wilder?"

"Pretty fucking good," he chuckles before Nixon pops into the screen behind him, looking a little more hungover than Ares.

"Hey, good twin. You should have been here. It was sick."

I inch up further on the couch without moving my foot or the ice pack. "Nix? What are you doing there?" And for a hot minute, I'm jealous of my brother for being in Kroydon Hills while I'm across the world.

Ares walks through a door, then shuts it behind him. "Nixon needed a place to crash last night, and Callen and Maddox were both otherwise occupied. He took one of my spare rooms. I think he's gonna stay here until he finds out where he's going in the draft next month."

Nix graduated from Boston University a few weeks ago. He's been staying with Mom and Dad, but we all know that's going to change after the pro hockey draft next month.

"And *you* weren't otherwise occupied?" I ask pointedly, even though I'm not sure I want to know. Definitely a glutton for punishment.

"Nah." He drops down onto a massive, messy bed, and I get a glance at his bare chest, and my heart aches. Well, maybe not just my heart. "Not my style. I just wanted to celebrate the win with my people." Those damn stormy eyes are stealing my soul through the screen, and I wonder silently if our timing will ever be right because six months later, I still want him. More now than ever before. "Besides, we're still celebrating the win. The owners are throwing a party tonight at Kingdom. You know, that hot bar in the city?" When I nod, he adds, "And the parade will be later this week. The celebration should go on for days."

"You sound like a busy man." I try unsuccessfully to stifle a yawn.

"Am I keeping you awake, Gracie?" His husky voice wraps around me like a blanket, comforting and warm, and my eyes grow heavier.

"Sorry. I took a pain pill earlier, and I think it's kicking in."

"A pain pill?" Concern laces his tone, and I want to kick myself for even mentioning it. "Are you okay?"

"It's nothing. I'm fine." My words are forced and hollow,

and I'm not sure if I'm trying to convince him or myself. The look he gives me lets me know I'm not doing a good job of either.

"Maybe you should take a night off."

I laugh quietly. "When was the last time *you* took a night off because you were sore?" He has the good graces to look mildly guilty. "That's what I thought. I know my body, and I know when to push it. I promise you, I'm okay."

"Maybe I should fly over there and make sure you're taking care of yourself."

Heat floods my cheeks at the thought of finally seeing Ares face-to-face again before it's replaced with annoyance. "Really? Don't you trust me to take care of myself? You're starting to sound just like everyone else."

"But I'm not anyone else, Grace." His voice is deep and growly . . . It's possessive and affects me in a way I'm too tired to think about but will definitely haunt my dreams.

I hear someone pound on Ares's door. "Dude. Let's go."

"Sounds like you better go," I whisper as I hold back another yawn.

Ares stares at me, seemingly frustrated before he licks his lower lip. "This conversation isn't over, Grace."

"You say that a lot, don't you, god of war?"

"Only where you're concerned, Grace."

"And why is that?" I whisper and close my eyes just for a moment, while I remember the last time Ares told me something wasn't over.

Apparently, he remembers too because that crooked, sexy smile spreads across his annoyingly handsome face. "Go sleep, tiny dancer. I'll talk to you soon."

The next day, I wake up to a text from my sister.

EVERLY
Why am I hearing from Ares that you're hurt?

What the hell?
He went to Everly?
I'm going to kill the little snitch.

GRACE
Because he's a man. They think any kind of pain is bad. They're all big babies. I twisted my ankle and had an ice pack on it the other day. That's all.

EVERLY
Why were you even talking to him?

Shit.

I never told Everly about the night of her wedding, and I've absolutely never mentioned the fact that I'm attracted to her husband's brother. Everly's a bit . . . hmmm . . . dramatic? I don't think it would go over well. It's one of the many reasons why I told him we're off-limits in the first place. I can only imagine how she'd flip out if we were together and how much worse it would be when we'd inevitably break up.

GRACE
I wanted to congratulate him on scoring the winning goal. That was awesome. Is Cross excited?

EVERLY

Yeah. It was pretty amazing. The whole city has been celebrating for days. Wish you were here.

GRACE

Me too. Miss you, sissy.

Ares

I slap my hand down on my nightstand, silencing my phone.

Fuck.

I'm not ready to wake up.

Feels like someone took a sledgehammer to my skull last night.

This is why I don't drink like this anymore.

The phone rings again, and I man up and answer.

"Hello," I rasp out.

"She's not hurt," a feminine voice snaps, and it sounds super fucking pissy.

I pull the phone away from my face and wipe the sleep from my eyes as I look at the screen. Damn it. *Everly*. "What are you talking about, blondie?"

"*My sister.*" Oh yeah. Definitely pissy.

It's too early for this shit.

"She's not hurt," she insists. "Her ankle was bothering her. That's normal for dancers."

"Normal doesn't make you take pain pills," I argue and drag a hand down my face. I need coffee. Or maybe a Red

Bull. "She was falling asleep on the phone. Over-the-counter shit doesn't do that."

"Don't make a big deal out of it, god of war. Dancers know their bodies. And Gracie is an elite athlete at the top of her game, just like you and Cross. She's a professional. She knows what she's doing." Everly's voice leaves no room for argument, like she thinks this is the end of the discussion, and I'm supposed to roll over now.

Does she know me at all?

I don't roll over.

Especially not where Grace is concerned.

She'll realize that at some point.

"Good talk, blondie," I groan.

"Grace has plenty of people to look out for her. She doesn't need you doing it too, Ares. Don't go getting any ideas about making my sister another notch on your bedpost."

What the fuck?

"Sure, Everly. Whatever you say." I crack my neck from side to side and groan . . . *again*. "Anything else you want to add, or are we done?"

"We're good," she tells me as if a switch flipped and now that she's set her boundaries, everything is good now. "See you for dinner this weekend."

"Yeah. Bye." I end the call and give up on any chance of sleeping off the rest of the hangover from hell.

Caffeine. I need caffeine and grease.

Lots of grease.

I wander down to the room Nixon basically moved into and bang on the door. "Sinclair, you want to get breakfast?"

The door to the room across the hall opens, and Bellamy sticks her head out. "Breakfast? You buying?"

"I can buy," comes from a female voice inside the same room.

"How did I not know you crashed here?" I lean against the doorframe and ask my sister, not really sure I want to know the answer.

Caitlin Beneventi opens the door and sashays around Bellamy and me on her way to the bathroom. "Because you were so drunk, Maddox and Nixon basically carried you to your room after the parade." She slams the bathroom door shut, and the fucking axe slams down against my skull for the final blow. I close my eyes and suck in a breath.

I may never drink again.

Bellamy laughs at my pain, like the little brat she likes to be.

"No luck finding your own place yet?"

"I was thinking," she starts off in her sweetest possible voice. Yeah, I'm about to get screwed. "Maybe I could grab your extra room for now."

"Nixon already claimed it." I pinch the bridge of my nose and close my eyes.

"He claimed *that* one." She points across the hall at the door Nixon finally opens. "What about this one?"

"You mean my office?" I ask, already knowing I'll say yes. Cross and I never could say no to Bellamy. That's what happens when your baby sister spends half her life in a hospital. You give her anything she wants. Most of the time, it was just for Cross or me to spend the night with her. She hates being alone. So we made sure she never was.

"Come on. You can't really call that an office. It has a futon, a desk, and a ton of boxes. Plus it's twice the size of my bedroom in Maine. *Please, Ares.* If you let us move in here—"

"Us?" I cut her off as Caitlin comes out of the bathroom and smiles at Nixon.

"Hi, roomie." She wiggles her fingers his way, then smiles at me. "Anybody in the mood for The Busy Bee? I could go for an eggs bene."

Bellamy looks up at me with big puppy-dog eyes, and I fold like a bad hand of poker.

Yesterday I went to bed with a three-bedroom condo all to myself, and somehow today, I woke up with three roommates.

What the fuck happened last night?

MADDOX

Did you actually let my sister move in with you?

ARES

Not sure she gave me much of a choice.

HENDRIX

She's always been kind of scary.

CALLEN

She's a hundred pounds soaking wet. How fucking scary can she be, you big bitch?

LEO

Pretty sure if I piss her off, she's going to slice off my balls with a knife she's hiding in her purse.

MADDOX

Nah. It's usually in her pocket.

ARES

What?

MADDOX

Don't worry. She's really good with it. She's got great aim with knives and guns.

CALLEN

Dude. Your dad let her move out?

MADDOX

Mom said he didn't have a choice.

CALLEN

Makes sense. Nobody wants to piss off your mom.

ARES

Why?

MADDOX

She's a better shot than Caitlyn.

ARES

Fuck me.

The Philly Press
KROYDON KRONICLES

IT'S GETTIN' HOT IN HERE

Hey, you beautiful people. It's summertime in the city, and it's getting HOT. The Wilder and Sinclair brothers were spotted last night at West End, celebrating the oldest Sinclair's recently signed contract with the Philadelphia Revolution. You heard it right here. The Sinclairs have traded in their football legacy for hockey skates. And while this reporter will miss the tight pants, the sheer testosterone on display between Ares Wilder, Cross Wilder, and his brother-in-law Nixon Sinclair, there's enough testosterone on the ice to make this reporter pant. And it definitely looked like I wasn't the only one panting last night. Remember, ladies, two of these three men are SINGLE.

#HotHockeyPlayers #NewFamilyLegacy #KroydonKronicles

ARES

"Get your ass moving, Sinclair." I pound on Nixon's door once before walking down the hall and grabbing my hockey bag. The season might be over, but practice never stops if you're smart. Let yourself get lazy in the offseason and you have to work twice as hard come time for training camp.

When I move into the kitchen, Bellamy is already sitting at the table with a mess of papers spread around her. I check my watch, then grab a bottle of water and stare at my sister. "What are you doing up so early?"

Bellamy looks up from a fat textbook and pushes her glasses on top of her head. "I've got a test this afternoon. Just trying to go over everything one more time." She lays her bright pink highlighter down and stares a little too closely at me. "The better question is, what are you up to, big brother?"

I cross my arms and wait because B hates it when someone doesn't answer her.

Drives her batshit crazy.

Waiting her out is the least painful way to find out what the fuck she's talking about because there's no way she knows what I'm actually up to, and I'd like to keep it that way.

My kid sister cocks her head to the side and smiles like a creepy psycho killer or something. "Your suitcase is packed and sitting next to your bed, and you told Cross yesterday you'd be coming to the beach later than the rest of us. So . . . where are you going, big brother?"

Why the fuck did I agree to roommates?

She's not even paying me rent.

"You watch too many true-crime shows, B."

She smiles proudly. "I could have been a detective."

Nixon walks into the kitchen and snags my water out of my hand. "Thanks, man. We ready to roll?"

"Yeah," I shove him back and grab another bottle from the fridge. "Let's go. We're meeting the guys at the practice rink in fifteen minutes."

"And . . ." Bellamy pushes.

"And I'll see you at the beach next week. Good luck on the test." I take a step out of the kitchen, and Nixon turns back to her.

"What'd I miss?" He grabs a piece of bacon from B's plate and pops it in his mouth.

"Ares is going somewhere this weekend when the rest of us are heading to the beach." She smacks Nix's hand when he moves in for a second piece of bacon. "Make your own."

Nixon catches up to me as I walk through the door. "Where are you going, god of war? You got a girl you haven't mentioned?"

If he only knew.

"Heading out to see a friend." That's all I'm willing to tell him.

"Is she a hot *friend*? More importantly, does she *have* hot friends?"

"Dude . . . Stop." It's nobody's business where I'm going or who I'm seeing, but telling my friends or my sister that is like throwing chum in shark-infested waters.

Nixon pushes the button for the elevator. "Whatever, man. How long you gone for?"

"I'm leaving after practice, and I'll catch you guys at the beach at the end of the week. Not sure when I'll get there." Guess it depends on how well my surprise goes over tonight.

"You're gonna miss the dinner Mom is throwing for Everly's birthday."

My first thought is, *if everything goes the way I want it to, you're goddamned right I will*—because I'll be celebrating it with her twin sister instead.

But since I can't say that to Nixon, I just shrug. "I'll bring a good gift."

"Where are you going anyway?"

"Where I should have gone six months ago."

"Hey, man. Bellamy says you're heading to the airport." I turn the volume up in my earbud and stare out the window at the plane I'm supposed to be boarding any minute as Cross checks up on me.

"Yeah, man. I was gonna tell you this morning at practice, but you no-showed. What's up with that?"

"Kerrigan gave us a stomach bug. She was puking all night, and Jaxon was puking all morning. If I left Everly with the two of them, she may have castrated me." Always the responsible one.

I love my brother and his family. But . . . yeah. "That sounds fucking awful."

"So where are you going?"

"To see a friend for a few days." The attendant announces first-class seating, and I'm saved by the bell. "Sorry, Cross. Gotta go. They just opened the gate. I'll see you at the beach. Kiss my niece and nephew for me when they feel better."

"Don't be stupid, brother," Cross warns.

"Never," I laugh and end the call.

When I get situated on the plane, I'm relieved to see the seat next to me open.

Hopefully, it stays that way.

I lean back, turn on a playlist, and close my eyes.

If the flight lands on time, I'll catch most of the show tonight.

I'm not sure how long I've been asleep when turbulence jolts the plane. *What the hell?* We drop again before a calm voice comes over the speaker. "We're currently experiencing a little turbulence due to a storm. The captain is taking us to a higher altitude, and it should be smooth sailing for the rest of the flight."

I look around and see an old guy next to me who looks like he's already knockin' on heaven's door. Dude's got to be ninety-five if he's a day, in an expensive gray suit with a navy-blue and yellow polka-dotted bow tie.

"Guess that woke you up there, Wilder." His shaky voice doesn't surprise me, but the fact he knows my name does. "Good. Maybe now, you'll stop snoring."

"Uhh . . . Have we met?" I know we haven't because I wouldn't forget this guy. He looks like Grandpa Carl from that Disney movie about the house and balloons Kerrigan loves. He just needs a yellow dog with a cone around his head.

I look around him to check for a walker covered in tennis balls.

Nope. Not there.

Okay. Guess that means it's not a dream.

"No." He watches me carefully. "But I've been a season ticket holder for the Revolution since I was a kid. You got a mean slapshot, kid. But you get in too many fights. You need to be more like that brother of yours."

Not the first time I've heard this.

"I'm the enforcer. It's my job to get into the fights Cross can't."

Who the fuck is this guy?

He scoffs, "If you say so."

"The team says so," I mumble. Why the hell am I arguing with this walking dinosaur?

"So, you going to London for business or pleasure, *enforcer*?" He says that last word like it's a curse he has to utter. When I don't answer, his leathery lips smile. "Ahh. You're going for a girl."

Grandpa Carl pulls out a butterscotch from his pocket and offers it to me.

Okay. I'll bite. I take the candy and pop it into my mouth. "Not just any girl."

This time, it's me smiling.

"We haven't seen each other in a few months. I'm surprising her tonight."

I've got no clue why the fuck I'm telling him any of this, but seriously, if he tried to sell it to *Sports Center*, who the hell would believe him anyway?

He pulls a deck of cards out of his other pocket and starts shuffling. "Does *not just any girl* have a name?"

I hesitate before answering, "Grace."

He places the deck on my drop-down table. "Cut the cards, Wilder."

I divide them in half and watch him finish shuffling before he deals us each a hand, puts the rest of the deck on the table, and flips the top card over.

"You ever play rummy?" he grumbles.

I nod. "We playing for money, old man?"

"Your mother ever teach you manners, kid? I've got a name."

"Wanna tell me what it is then, since you know mine?" I pick up a card and drop another one down.

He does the same with his cards. "It's Carl."

I choke back my laugh. Grandpa. Fucking. Carl.

I wonder if Gracie likes that movie. Seems like something she'd like.

"So you going to tell me about your girl, kid?" I look at his weathered hands and see him play with a plain, gold wedding band on his ring finger. "How long have you and Grace been together?"

I shift in my seat and pick up another card. "We're not really together—not yet."

"Why the hell not?"

"She's a ballerina in London, and it's not like my job can transfer me over there. We've been taking our time. Getting to know each other better. It's complicated."

"You young people are all the same. You think it's going to be easy. You think the universe owes you something, and the perfect girl is going to fall into your lap. That it's all going to be smooth sailing after that." He laughs, then coughs and wipes his mouth with a handkerchief he pulls from his pocket.

How much shit can he fit in his pockets?

"It doesn't work that way. You've got to decide whether she's worth the work. If she is, you make it work because before you know it, something bigger than you can take her away permanently. And when that happens, and you only have memories, you won't be grateful you took your time living in two different countries. You'll wish you had one more day holding hands. One more dinner sitting across from her. One more night with her in your arms. Don't waste time, kid. It's the only thing you can never get more of."

Holy shit.

Those words hit me like a Mack truck going ninety miles an hour.

"Take it from someone who knows, kid. Don't ever waste time."

Grace

> **EVERLY**
> Are you sure you can't come home this week?

> **GRACE**
> I'm sure.

> **EVERLY**
> Not even for a few days?

> **GRACE**
> Sorry, sissy. I'm back to the flat after the show tonight, and I might just sleep for a week.

> **EVERLY**
> What if I put Kerrigan on the phone?

> **GRACE**
> Using your daughter to guilt me isn't fair, Everly. Lennon is going to her parents' country home for the week, which means I have the flat to myself. I've got Aunt Nattie's last three books sitting on my Kindle, and I plan on drinking a bottle of wine and falling in love with my next Natalie Sinclair book boyfriend. I don't care if I see a single soul this week.

EVERLY
Lennon is going home. Why can't you?

> **GRACE**
> Her family is sending a helicopter. She'll be on it for thirty minutes. Not the same thing.

EVERLY
But it's our birthday . . .

> **GRACE**
> It is, and you'll be spending it with your incredibly sexy husband and beautiful kids.

EVERLY
He is sexy, isn't he?

I shake my head and smile at my sister. I miss her like I'd miss a limb.

> **GRACE**
> Love you, bad twin.

EVERLY
Miss you, good twin.

"A word, Miss Sinclair?" Jeffrey Jenkins, our director,

startles me as he crosses the dressing room. He was a star twenty years ago. A visionary dancer with more natural skill and grace in his fingertips than most people could ever hope to have in their entire bodies. What he doesn't have now, and probably didn't have then, was patience, tact, or respect for the women he works with.

"Yes, Mr. Jenkins?" I look up at him through the reflection in the mirror as he moves behind me. His hands rest on my shoulders, and my stomach drops.

This man's touch always lingers a little too long. He skates the line between appropriate and *inappropriate* without ever actually crossing it. But it leaves an ugly feeling in my gut all the same.

"How are you feeling tonight? How's the foot?" His voice is smooth and calm, and it hides the anger that lies just beneath the surface. When my pas-de-deux partner dropped me this morning during practice, that anger was right there, bubbling over, and it was directed solely at me.

"It's fine," I answer quickly. I've learned short and sweet are the best ways to handle any conversations with Jenkins because he doesn't actually care about your answer, so long as it's the one he wants to hear.

"I expect you to rest that foot this week, Miss Sinclair. You've been distracted these past few weeks. You can't afford distractions." His eyes travel over me, and I force myself not to flinch. "I expect once you're rested, you'll be able to give me the 100 percent I demand of all my dancers. You've been lacking lately." He lifts a brow, and I school my features to hide my shock.

"Yes, sir. One hundred percent, sir."

"Hundreds of dancers would give anything to be in the position you're in, Grace."

My nerves threaten to revolt at the use of my first name.

He never calls me Grace. It's always Miss Sinclair. "Yes, sir. I'm aware."

A finger trails along my neck, and I shiver. Judging by Jenkins's smile, he thinks that's a good reaction.

It's not.

I've heard rumors of him dating his ballerinas, if dating is what it can really be called, but he's never indicated he expected that from me.

"I'd hate to have to consider one of the other girls for the part I've got earmarked for you."

"Gracie . . ." Lennon calls out as she walks into the dressing room. "Hey." She looks between Jenkins and me. "Charles is looking for you."

I blow out a breath I hadn't realized I was holding and stand from my chair. "Thanks, Lennon. I'll be right there."

Jenkins takes a step back as I move around him. "Looks like we've got a show to do."

"Remember what I said, Miss Sinclair."

I nod and walk away.

How could I forget?

The life of a ballerina always looked so glamorous to me.

The beautiful costumes.

The stunning sets.

The perfection the dancers produced with their bodies. The way the graceful arc of their arm could bring tears to my eyes, or the perfect lift could make me hold my breath, watching the pair in perfect sync.

As a little girl, I loved everything about it.

As I grew up, I loved that I was good at it. That it gave me a path to follow.

Now as an adult, I stand here on this stage with a beautiful bouquet of long-stemmed red roses in my arms and an entire theater on their feet for a standing ovation, and I don't feel anything. I'm numb.

I've lost my true north.

Mom used to say it was that spot you find to focus on in every studio, on every stage.

Your constant. Your balance. Your anchor as you're whipping out countless flawless pirouettes. You spin your head quickly and focus on your spot with each new revolution, so you don't lose your balance and fall.

But... I've lost my balance.

I'm still going through the motions, but... everything *just is.* And the overwhelming relief that this performance is over gives new life to my lungs and carries much-needed oxygen through my blood.

I need to get out of here.

The curtains close, and the stage lights dim as everyone hugs and congratulates each other on the successful run of a beautiful show. But I'm going to hyperventilate if I don't get out of here.

Chatter starts immediately. Discussions about everyone's plans for their week off. But my vision darkens. Adrenaline still courses through everyone's veins as I bump into members of the corps, trying desperately to get back to the quiet dressing room before the tears that are threatening fall without my permission.

And I almost make it too.

"Ms. Sinclair," our stage manager, June, stops me just as I put my hand on the doorknob. Well she tries to, but I keep moving on autopilot, desperately needing to get out of here. "Excuse me, Ms. Sinclair."

Damn it.

Manners bred into me my entire life insist I turn around.

With a practiced smile in place, I turn to face her. Only something... *someone* catches my eye at the end of the hall.

Is that—?

I think my heart might actually skip a beat when his smile spreads across that handsome face.

"There's someone here asking to see you, Ms. Sinclair. He says—"

I don't wait for June to finish before I move.

"Ares?"

He slides past the security guard in time to catch me as I leap for him, and the first tear finally falls.

Two strong arms wrap around me like a vice grip, and my feet dangle in the air as I bury my face in his neck and try not to cry. "What are you doing here?"

"I promised you I'd see you dance in this show, and I don't break my promises." His arms tighten around me, and I feel it right away. "I missed you so damn much, Grace."

The comfort.

The relief.

It feels like...

Home.

I hang on for dear life because that's what he is right now. A lifeline. "I can't believe you came," I whisper through the tears that won't stop now that they've started.

"There's nowhere else I'd rather be." He lowers me to my feet and picks up a beautiful bouquet of wildflowers he must have dropped when I launched myself at him.

Oh well.

"Come with me." I lace my fingers with his and tug him behind me into the dressing room. Dancers stop us every few steps, congratulating me on the performance, before we make it to the dressing room for the principal dancers.

I guide him next to my mirror and just stare for a minute. "I can't believe you're really here..."

This man... standing in front of me in a custom-fitted navy-blue suit with a crisp white shirt, the first few buttons unbuttoned. *My goodness*... I run my hand down his lapel and realize this is the first time in weeks I've felt anything at all.

"Let me take you out to dinner tonight." He crosses his thick arms over his chest, and I just stare stupidly for a beat until he clears his throat. "Come on, good twin. I flew all day to see you. Don't make me beg."

"My flat is a ten-minute walk from here, and my roommate is leaving right from here for a week with her parents at their country house. There's a pub beneath my place with pretty shitty food, but it makes for easy takeout. You willing to stay in instead, god of war?"

"You had me at *your flat*."

ARES

I follow Grace through a creaky back door into the alley behind the theater as I shoulder my bag and hers. "I need to stop by the hotel and check in first."

Grace stops and turns. Her beautiful aqua eyes widen as her dark hair hangs in soft waves around her face. "You haven't checked in yet?"

"No." The urge to touch her again is so damn strong, it's hard to keep my hands to myself. Texts and FaceTime haven't cut it since she left. But I force my feet not to move and my hands to stay put. "I came right here. I was cutting it close and didn't want to miss the beginning of the show." I shift my bag. "I've got everything I need in here."

She cocks her pretty head to the side, staring at me as a dimple pops deep in her flushed cheek.

I fucking love when this girl blushes.

She and Everly may be identical twins, but from the minute I met her, she was all I saw.

"Or you could just stay with me." Her flush burns brighter as she bites down on her plump bottom lip, and my dick jumps behind my zipper. "I mean, you could crash in Lennon's room. It's not like she'll be using it or anything."

I press my thumb against her lip, forcing it free, and drag the pad of my thumb across.

Fuck, I want this woman.

"You sure, good twin? I've got a reservation ten minutes from here. I wouldn't want to scandalize you," I tease.

Her long, dark lashes kiss her cheeks, then she blinks up at me before nodding. "Maybe I'd like that."

Tension clings to the humid air quietly surrounding us.

Grace grips the front of my shirt in shaking hands and tugs me to her. "I still can't believe you're here."

I can't believe it took me so damn long to get here.

I cup her cheek and press my lips to her head, inhaling her citrusy scent.

Man, I missed that smell.

"I was always coming for you, Grace." I lift her face to mine, and her expressive eyes sparkle and darken as her pretty pink lips part, and she sucks in a breath. My thumb skims over her cheek. "Just you . . ."

Grace presses up on her toes, closing what little space there is between us. "I missed you," she whispers and leans in.

She jumps back when the door to the alley slams open against the brick wall with a loud bang, followed by a group of dancers spilling out into the alley.

The sheer disappointment in Grace's eyes makes me smile.

Yeah . . . she feels this too.

The pull is just as powerful tonight as it was that night in Kroydon Hills.

More powerful, if that's possible.

I wrap an arm around her delicate frame. "Let's get out of here."

She leans into me wordlessly.

"Lead the way, tiny dancer."

*I*t doesn't take long to get to her place. And she wasn't kidding—she lives above a pub that looks like the city was built up around it over a few hundred years. From the outside, it doesn't look like much. But as we climb the stairs to her flat, I realize how wrong my assumption was. It's deceptively large inside. High-end furniture is mixed with an eclectic mash-up of vintage and, I'm pretty sure, hand-made pieces. Soft looking pink blankets drape over the small couch and both chairs, and similar throw pillows are scattered around.

This gorgeous girl spins in a circle with her arms out and her smile wide. "It's not much, but it's mine." She points to one side of the room . . . and the more I look, the more I realize it's a very pink room. "Your bedroom and bathroom are over there. Kitchen is behind me." She moves in front of me and stops. "And my bedroom and bathroom are behind you. I'm going to jump in the shower."

I drop both bags to the floor. "You sure you don't mind me crashing here, good twin?"

Her hands press against my chest, and she nods. "How long are you staying?" Her voice is quiet and hesitant, like she's holding her breath as she waits for the answer.

The tension between us is running hot and heavy and building higher with each passing minute.

I run a hand over her long brown hair and tug. *Fuck me.* I want her so goddamned bad. "I promised Cross I'd meet them at the beach at the end of the week. I'm supposed to leave after your birthday."

"Really?" Her eyes light up, and there goes that blush again. "You'll be here for my birthday?"

"I sent someone to record your opening night, just so I could see it, Grace. And you're surprised I'm here for your birthday?"

Her hands slide up from my chest around my neck, and blood roars in my ears when she moves closer. "Seven months is a long time, god of war."

She's got no fucking clue.

"And we never made any promises. I saw the pictures. I guess I'm just still shocked you're here." Grace holds perfectly still as her eyes skim over my face. "I thought maybe we missed our chance."

"That wasn't our chance. That was our test," I growl.

"Did we pass?" she asks with the sexiest smile.

"Yeah, baby, we passed. And if you keep looking at me that way, I'm going to trace every inch of that fucking blush on your cheeks all the way down your body with my tongue, tiny dancer. Now go shower so I can act like I'm a gentleman for a little longer before I show you exactly how much I missed you."

Grace steps back and pulls her sweater over her head, dropping it on the floor and leaving her standing in front of me in charcoal gray sweatpants, Ugg boots, and a tiny black tank top. Her breasts are plumped up and threatening to pop right out of that tank, and my mouth waters, absolutely desperate to get my first taste of my girl. She moves across the room, then turns back, a sexy little smile spreading across her face. "How can you miss something you never had?"

"Oh, baby . . . Don't doubt for one single minute that you haven't been mine since the snowstorm."

"Looked like you might have been someone else's the night you won the Cup." Her chin juts up defiantly, like she's daring me to correct her. Good twin has claws. I like it. "I saw the pictures the *Kroydon Kronicles* shared, Ares. It's okay, you know. I didn't expect you not to date."

I cross the room in two strides and wrap a hand around her neck possessively as I press her back against the wall. Because that's what I want—to possess this woman. To protect her. To fucking worship her. "There were lots of people at that bar, baby. And everyone wanted our attention. But not a single one of them was the woman I wanted because you were across a goddamned ocean. So I waited until I could get here."

Grace sucks in a breath.

"Seven fucking months, Grace. Seven months I've waited. There hasn't been anyone else. Not a single woman. Not since that night. No one but you," I growl, tired of this shit. "I'm here for one fucking reason."

"And what's the reason?" she asks, a little shaken, and slowly drags her teeth over her trembling lower lip.

I press my thumb over her thrumming pulse, and her gorgeous aqua eyes close as the tension in her shoulders tightens.

"You really don't know, baby?" With a hand on her hip, I squeeze until she looks at me. "You're the reason. Every call. Every text. Every voice memo and every video. Fuck, Gracie. It's you. I haven't been able to get your voice out of my head. Your face out of my mind. I never stopped thinking about you. Or stopped wondering what you're doing, and who you're doing it with. I've been the good guy for months. I gave you the space to figure out what you wanted. I'm not the good guy, Gracie. And I'm done waiting. I'm here for you."

Her lips form a perfect little O.

"You never said anything," she whispers.

"I couldn't say anything, Grace. You needed time." I slide

my palm to her cheek, and she nuzzles her face into it as she practically purrs.

She turns her face slightly and presses her lips against my palm. "I would have rather had you."

"Fuck, Grace. Don't tell me that," I groan. "I had a plan. I was going to be a gentleman."

"There was this one guy . . . a dancer from the troupe. He asked me out a few months ago, and Lennon convinced me to go."

My jaw clenches, thinking of my girl with anyone else, and I pull her close, ready to make sure no one else can ever doubt who her man is.

"But five minutes after we got to the restaurant, I knew I didn't want to be there. Not with him." She lifts her face higher, and the moonlight catches her eyes. "Aren't you going to ask me how I knew, Ares?"

"You gonna tell me?" I push her.

"He wasn't you. And even though I keep reminding myself of all the reasons you and I can't be together . . . all the complications we have, I still wanted him to be you." She lifts up on her toes and presses her forehead to mine. "We're a really bad idea, god of war."

"We're the best fucking decision I've ever made."

Grace

Ares lifts me from the floor, and I wrap myself around him as he presses me against the wall and pushes my hair away from my face. "Tell me to stop, Gracie . . ."

I lean into his touch, wondering if I'm dreaming because I swear I've heard those words a million times, but I always wake up right before anything happens. "I think I'll die if you stop."

I gasp as his lips hover over mine. My nearly nonexistent defenses weaken and wither. "Please, Ares . . ."

Ares slides his hand up my neck and digs into my hair. His eyes fix on mine, sending a sharp, sweet bolt of hunger coursing through my veins before his mouth finally claims mine.

The world stands still, cocooning us as it implodes, leaving only us. Only now.

His tongue licks into my mouth, and I moan as electricity sparks and spikes. My body burns while his erection grows thicker between my legs.

Our tongues dance a slow dance. Learning. Exploring. Setting every single nerve ending on fire. Spreading like a wildfire, ready to engulf everything it touches.

I dig my nails into the ridiculous muscles in his shoulders and shift my hips, needing friction. Desperate to feel his skin. His heat. His weight.

"Ares . . . I need . . ."

"Honey . . . I'm home." I look up to see Lennon standing in the doorway and looking horrified.

"Oh my God," I whisper.

"Well, now." Lennon walks in and shuts the door. "I guess I'd have stayed home, too, if I knew this giant of a man would be here waiting for me."

"Grace?" Ares asks as I wiggle out of his hold and slide my legs down.

"Ares, meet Lennon." Ares discreetly adjusts himself before turning to meet Lennon. "My roommate."

He offers her his hand, then turns to look at me. "Wait . . . aren't you . . . ?"

Lennon rolls her eyes. "Yup. That's me. You'd think they wouldn't fuck up sending the helicopter for me. But I guess since I'm not in the top ten in line for the throne, I don't rank." Lennon drops her bag on the couch and moves into the kitchen. "Did you order dinner yet? I'm starving."

Ares's eyes keep bouncing between Lennon and me, like he can't figure out what's happening here.

"She doesn't like to acknowledge the whole princess thing." I try to hide my laughter as I lean into him. "Look at it this way. Now you can't sleep in Lennon's room."

He tucks a lock of hair behind my ear. "I wasn't sleeping there anyway, good twin."

GRACE

**Self-care isn't a luxury. It's a necessity.
I'm making myself a priority.**
—Grace's secret thoughts

Turns out there was an issue with the helicopter, so Lennon's family is sending a car tomorrow. I can't decide if she's thrilled or annoyed.

"So this is the infamous Ares." She pushes her plate back and rests her chin on her fist. At the moment, she's definitely leaning toward thrilled. "You know . . . you look much bigger on the ice."

I kick her under the table and smile when she flinches.

"Fine." She purses her lips together and cocks a pretty red brow. "You don't. But honestly, the way Gracie drools over your games, I half expected you to be a real god. But I guess you're close enough to a chiseled Greek one."

"Lennon," I gasp, and Ares chokes on his beer.

See? Perks of living above a pub.

Did I mention Lennon's uncle owns the pub? And maybe half the street?

"Whatever, Grace. You watch all his games. You don't really expect me to think it's for his brother, do you?" She sips her red wine and leans back in her chair as I die of absolute mortification. "Not that your brother isn't hot. But you know, the whole *married to her twin* kinda ruins that fantasy. Besides . . . it looks like you're Cross 2.0, only bigger . . . and maybe hotter." She waves her hand in front of her face and glances my way conspiratorially before looking back at Ares. "So what are your intentions with our Grace, Mr. Wilder?"

"Oh my God." I throw my napkin across the table at her. This has gotten completely out of control. "Stop it," I squeal. "I'm nobody's Grace," I chastise Lennon while simultaneously wondering if I could get away with smothering her in her sleep . . . her bodyguard probably would have an issue with that. But it's not like she sleeps in our flat with us. Maybe she wouldn't know . . .

"That's not what it looked like when I walked in," Lennon interrupts my quickly spiraling thoughts. Maybe that's a sign I've watched enough serial killer podcasts this month.

Heat creeps up my cheeks, and I take the bottle of red wine out of her hands. "I think you're cut off for tonight. When did you say you're going home?"

"Don't be such a bore, Gracie girl." She snags the wine back and fills both our glasses. "Daddy said they're sending a car tomorrow. God forbid I spend any downtime here. But part of the deal when they agreed to let me come here to dance was that I have to come home whenever I can." She sips her wine and peers over the glass at me. "You guys could always come with me . . ."

I shake my head. I've already told her no every other day for at least a week.

Self-care.

That's all I'm concerned with this week.

At least I was until Ares walked into that hall.

"What are your plans for the week? Going to take Ares sightseeing?"

"I don't know. We haven't really talked about it." I look over at Ares, and heat blooms for a whole new reason. My God. The way his hands felt on my body . . . That may be my new idea of self-care.

"I'll do anything you want, good twin." A devious smile slides across Ares's face.

"Ohh . . . Good answer, hockey god," Lennon snarks, and she's not wrong.

That was a great answer.

"Well . . ." She stands from the table and grabs our plates. "I'm going to shower and go to bed." I can tell from the evil little glint in her eye she's about to throw a zinger my way. "Just saying . . . I'll be wearing noise-canceling headphones tonight. So, you know . . . feel free to make some noise."

Oh. My. God.

"I'm going to kill her," I mumble under my breath as her bedroom door closes before I drop my head into my hands, utterly exhausted from the ups and downs of this day.

"Pretty sure you can't kill royalty." Ares tugs me into his lap and massages my neck with one big hand. "You didn't mention that your roommate was a princess."

"She doesn't like to make a big deal of it and refuses to use her title." I sigh dramatically. "Besides, her bodyguard likes me more than her. I really think I could get away with it if I wanted to."

"He probably wants to fuck you." Ares eyes dare me to tell him he's wrong.

"First of all, *he's* a she. And *she* is very much interested in men. So you're wrong, Mr. Wilder." I yawn and lean my head against his shoulder. "Did I thank you for coming tonight?"

"You don't ever need to thank me for wanting to see you, Grace." He stands with me in his arms like I weigh nothing. So freaking sexy. "Ready for bed, tiny dancer?"

A warmth envelops me, and I circle my arms around his neck and yawn again. "You know I can walk, right?"

Ares walks across our flat into my bedroom and carefully sits me down on the bed, then drags his big hand down his face and over his sexy scruff. An internal war wages behind his dark eyes. "Do you mind if I take a shower? I need to wash the airplane funk off before bed."

Ares Wilder is going to be naked in my shower.

How many times have I touched myself in there, thinking about him?

So many . . . too many to count.

And now I'm hot for a whole different reason.

Down girl.

Ares reaches down and runs his knuckles over my cheek. "Where'd you just go? Your whole face just warmed up."

I shake my head from side to side and smile. "Nowhere important. Just thinking about the shower."

"Whatever you say, good twin."

He turns toward my bathroom, and I consider following behind him—considering taking a second shower for the night. "Hey, Ares . . ."

I want to ask if he'd mind some company, then I see the picture of Everly and me from her wedding . . . to Ares's brother. This is such a bad idea.

When he turns and smiles that wicked smile, I chicken out. "Towels are in the closet."

Ares

Jacking off in my shower to images of Grace has become part of my routine. That's what happens when you go from being a healthy, sexually active adult male to fantasizing about the perfect girl a million miles away. You jack off. A. Lot.

Do I want to fuck Grace Sinclair?

Unequivocally, yes.

Do I want to stuff her full of my fingers, my tongue, my dick, and make her writhe until she screams my name and her voice is hoarse?

Fuck yes.

Is any of that going to happen tonight?

No. No, it's not.

Because that's not what tonight was supposed to be about. Lennon coming home was a good thing. Even if it's a little strange that the King of Elwyn's niece shares a flat with Grace.

How the fuck does no one back home know that little fact?

But ignoring the royalty in the other room, her interruption forced us to take a breather and not jump right into bed tonight. Even if that's all I want to do.

Grace and I need time. Not more time apart, though, just time to get on the same page. *When in the actual hell did I start sounding like a girl?* Next, I'll start talking about feelings. *Fuck.* I don't know how to do this. I've never been in a relationship. I've never been with a woman for longer than a few weeks. And those were few and far between. Even the word *relationship* creeps me the fuck out. At least it used to. Now, it just seems . . . right.

Everything about Grace seems to fit.

She's it.

She's all I think about . . . My obsession.

Her sultry smile. Her soft hair. Her flawless fucking tits that are gonna fit so perfectly in my mouth. *Fuck*. I groan and stroke it fast. *Harder*. Until I'm imagining Grace beneath me. Her tits bouncing with each thrust of my cock. Nails scoring my skin. My mouth on her skin. Tasting her.

Fuck . . .

I come surrounded by Grace's scent under the hot spray, her face the only thing I see as my eyes close.

When I step back into her room a few minutes later, she's changed into a pale-pink baby tee with black swirling font stretched across her boobs that says *Ballet – like a sport, only harder*. It hits just above her belly button, leaving a bare strip of toned soft skin I want to lick. Grace is sitting with her knees bent on the bed. Tiny black sleep shorts ride high on her thighs, and glasses I didn't know she wears are perched on her nose as she looks at her Kindle.

"What'cha reading?" I grip the doorframe above my head and lean forward, liking the sexy, sleepy look on her face when she lifts her head my way.

"My aunt's newest book." She closes her case and pushes her black glasses into her long hair like a headband. Her eyes drag over my chest, and I doubt she even realizes she licks her lips. How is it possible a woman so naturally sexy can be so incredibly unaware.

"The aunt who has the show on Netflix?"

Grace doesn't answer. She just licks her lips, nods, and hums, "Hmm . . ."

"Think I can get a pillow and blanket for the couch?"

She tosses her Kindle to her nightstand. "Oh, come on. Like you're going to fit on my couch. My bed is big enough for the two of us." She pushes her feet under the blanket and wraps her arms around her bent knees.

"I don't know, good twin . . . You think you can keep your

hands to yourself if I get in that bed? We're talking about my reputation, after all. I'd hate for you to think less of me in the morning."

Her laughter lights up the room as she tosses back the blanket. "You're such a goofball."

"But a respectable one," I tell her as I sit down next to her. "Pretty sure we've been here before, tiny dancer."

"Seems like déjà vu, doesn't it, god of war?"

I wrap an arm around her, and she rests her head against my chest.

"We're still a bad idea, Ares."

Acid churns in my gut with her words. "Give me one good reason."

"I'll give you two—my sister and your brother." Even while she argues with me, her body relaxes, and she drapes an arm across my chest. "They're going to give us so much shit."

"So we don't tell them," I say, even though the words make me angrier than I thought they could. "Not yet. Not until we figure things out for ourselves."

"Okay, how about the fact you live with my brother? Pretty sure that's another reason," she argues.

"Sweetheart, your brother lives with me. So does my sister and Caitlin. And I'm not asking any of them for their opinions on my life. You shouldn't either." My fingers draw lazy circles on her hip, just above her shorts, and I was right —her skin is so fucking soft.

"We haven't even talked about the fact we live on opposite sides of the world . . . Like I said . . . we're a terrible idea, Ares."

I lift her chin so she's looking at me. "So we'll have to work for it. You don't get to the levels you and I are at by being scared of hard work. Have you ever had anything great that was easy, baby? Because I'm a big believer that the harder the work, the sweeter the reward."

And I have no doubt that Grace Sinclair will be the sweetest reward I could ever earn.

"How can you be so sure?" she whispers in the dark room, and a chill snakes down my spine.

"Because the first time I met you, I knew you were mine."

GRACE

**The scariest thing about crazy girls is they usually run in packs.
If you think I'm a lot by myself, you should see me with my friends.**
—Grace's secret thoughts.

EVERLY

Can someone please remind me that sandy sex is a no-go next time I decide a late-night walk on the beach with my husband sounds like a good idea?

GRACIE

Eww, Evie! You seriously haven't learned your lesson yet?

LINDY

Hey – I watched your kids so you could have that sandy sex. Suck it up buttercup and go take a shower.

BRYNLEE

What I wouldn't give to have sand problems.

GRACIE

Same.

LINDY

I mean . . . sand problems can be fun if done right. Easton likes to help me get rid of the sand after. That shower alone makes the sandy sex worth it.

KENZIE

Eww. We're talking about sex, right? Sex and my brother . . . Can we not? Please . . .

Also - you DO NOT even want me to tell you about all the ways dirty, sandy sex can wreak havoc on your body. Ten out of ten, this doctor says no.

BRYNLEE

You've got to loosen up, Kenz. Seriously. You don't know what you're missing out on.

EVERLY

Kenzi, I haven't had nearly enough coffee to be lectured about dying by dick today.

LINDY

I thought I was going to choke once. But I relaxed and swallowed, and I definitely didn't die.

KENZIE

You're really never going to stop torturing me, are you?

LINDY

Nope. It's way too much fun.

BRYNLEE

We miss you, Kenz. It's not the same without Gracie and you.

GRACIE

> I see how it is. I'm an afterthought now. LOL

KENZIE

I moved out two weeks ago, Grace. You've been gone for six months.

BRYNLEE

All you bitches left me alone in this giant condo. I think it might be time to find my own place. Or at the very least, a dog.

EVERLY

Really? There's a house around the corner from us that just went on the market.

BRYNLEE

Not sure I want a whole house yet.

EVERLY

Fine. You're no fun, Brynn.

LINDY

Lenny and Bash's bulldog should be having babies soon. You should get one.

BRYNLEE

Maybe

GRACIE

> Kenz - How is DC?

KENZIE

The hospital is great. The surgeons are incredible. I love it. But I miss Kroydon Hills.

LINDY

When do you think you'll make it home?

KENZIE

They made all the residents sign an eighty-hour a week contract. We're only entitled to three days off a month. You might see me in five years.

EVERLY

Don't say that. Gracie never comes home. You can't be nonexistent too.

GRACIE

No more guilt trips, Evie. I feel bad enough.

EVERLY

Then come home for our birthday, sissy.

BRYNLEE

Don't make her feel worse than she already does, Evie.

LINDY

Enjoy your week off, Grace. We'll be there to visit at the end of the summer.

KENZIE

Just got paged. Gotta go. Love you guys.

BRYNLEE

You got this, Kenz. Go slice open brains.

KENZIE

Not exactly how it works.

I can't help the laughter that bubbles up.

"You ready to show me your city, good twin? I got us a private pod for the London Eye tonight. You've got five hours to fill with fun, touristy shit before our reservation."

I turn to find Ares standing in my living room. Worn blue jeans hang from his hips and showcase powerful thighs. A soft, gray t-shirt stretches across his broad shoulders and over his massive chest, and holy hell . . . a backward ball cap the same color as his dark eyes is sitting on his head like the cherry on top of a deliciously sexy sundae.

Damn. He's a pretty package.

My eyes jump down to his actual package, and I look away.

Yup. That's impressive in those jeans too.

I throw on my cross-body bag and grab my keys. Lennon was picked up a few hours ago, leaving Ares and me alone. I didn't have the heart to tell him I don't really feel like sightseeing. I just wanted to stretch and rest today. But I can do that tomorrow instead. "Ready."

"Come on. We've got time to stop by Westminster Abbey before we have to be in line at the London Eye. Our reservation is for eight." I link my arm through Ares and rest my head on his shoulder as we stroll slowly through the city.

Ares hasn't noticed that my foot's been bothering me, or at the very least, he's been kind enough not to say anything about our slow pace today. We did a lot of hopping on and off the double-decker tour bus that took us around the city, so I was able to rest it then. I doubt he noticed it was swollen under my maxi dress.

Other than the slight throb in my ankle, the day has been a little slice of heaven. Ares and I had never done anything alone before the night of Everly's wedding. We were always surrounded by our friends and family. That never left for much of a chance to get to know each other. But once I left and our texts and calls started, that all changed. Today might have been the first time we spent a day together, but it felt like I was with my best friend. I'm not sure exactly when that happened.

"Tell me your favorite thing about living in this city."

I think about that for a minute. Really think about it before I answer.

"The lack of expectations. No one expects me to fit in a perfect little box here. No one has known me since I was born. No one knows my family. There are no preconceived ideas about who I am or who I need to be. Back home, it's different. *Not bad.* Just different." I look around at the people mulling around us. "There's a kind of freedom here that I love."

"What about dance?"

"What about it?" I look up at him and run my fingers along his clenched jaw. "What's wrong?"

"I don't like that you felt that way in Kroydon Hills," he growls, and that sound does crazy things to my body. "You should always feel free, Grace."

"It wasn't always bad. But the pressure can be a lot to deal with." I shrug, not wanting to overthink too hard. "It's just different now."

"Do you ever think about what comes next? What does life look like after ballet?"

"No." My answer is automatic.

It's a short answer to a complicated question.

It's also a lie.

I think about it every day.

Because I don't know if I want to keep doing this to myself anymore.

But I don't have any idea what else is out there or what comes next.

Is it possible to have a midlife crisis at twenty-six?

I don't want to know the answer, so I spin the question. "What about you, god of war? Are you making Kroydon Hills a permanent thing? Do you want to stay with the Revolution until you retire?"

We stop in front of the ancient abbey, beautiful and lit up under the starry sky. It's awe-inspiring and humbling with its hundreds of years of history behind those doors.

Ares brushes a lock of hair over my shoulder, and goosebumps skip over my skin as he cups my face in his hands. "I'll stay with the Revolution as long as they'll have me. I'm hoping I can retire there. I could see staying in Kroydon Hills if the reason to stay was there."

"Yeah . . ." I trail off because I get it. This day has been amazing. Too good to be true. And that's because it is . . . too good to be true. Nothing this good can last. No matter what he wants to believe. We have no future. Not while we live on two different continents.

But I refuse to let that negativity ruin such an amazing day.

I look up at the abbey. "It's beautiful, isn't it?"

"Yeah . . . beautiful."

When I turn my head, he's looking at me, not the abbey.

This man . . .

He captures my lips with his, and I melt in his arms. "I'm not giving up on us, Grace."

I wrap my arms around his waist and soak in his warmth, unable to bring myself to tell him there isn't an us to hold on to. Let me live in the fantasy for a few more days.

Thirty minutes later, the attendant is letting us on our pod, and I realize just how high this thing is, up close and personal. Lennon tried to get me on it when I first moved here last winter, but I think it snowed, and we stayed in, binging *The Kings Of Kroydon Hills* on Netflix instead.

I lean across Ares as we enter our glass pod. "Excuse me. Exactly how high up does this go?"

Ares laughs at me as the attendant answers, "Four hundred and forty-three feet, ma'am."

The door shuts behind us, and I stand in the center of the pod, feeling a little queasy.

"Scared?" Ares teases.

I side-eye him while I move in front of the windows and try to put on a brave face. "Maybe a little."

A few minutes later, we begin our ascent, and my stomach drops.

"I've got you," he whispers as he stands behind me. His reflection stares back in the dark glass in front of us.

Ares Wilder is taller than mortal men, fitting for the god of war. I'm five-seven, and he makes me look tiny. He's well over six feet. Probably closer to six-five. And those muscles . . . they do lovely things for his appearance. He should be on the cover of a magazine or walking a runway somewhere.

He leans a hand against the window, over my shoulder, and watches London pass around us. Heat radiates off him, and my body anticipates the touch that doesn't come.

With each inch we rise higher into the inky night's sky, my heart races and my pulse pounds. I try to convince myself it's the height and not the man, until I step back and bump into him, and my stomach jumps. "Heights don't typically bother me."

"Relax, Gracie. You're safe with me."

Ares's voice washes over me, deep and rumbly, and I momentarily forget where we are.

And who we are.

An arm wraps around my waist, anchoring me to him, and I'm pulled back against his chest, safe and warm. *Protected*.

Ares drags his nose along the column of my neck, and I rest my head back against his shoulder. "I bet I could help you relax," he whispers into my ear.

It's the way his voice dances over my skin.

The promise it holds.

It's intoxicating.

His big hand possessively slides over my hip and stops at the thigh-high slit in my dress. Calloused fingers slip between the soft fabric and my bare skin. They're rough against my thigh, and my breath catches with the first touch. Anticipation tingles through every inch of my overheated skin, and I forget that we're nearly four hundred feet above the ground. I become blissfully ignorant of the glass surrounding us that can clearly be seen through. I focus on him. On his rough fingers and warm breath. On the strength of his chest and the way he makes me feel.

It's a heady experience and not something I'm used to.

"Tell me you want this, Grace." His other hand slides around my throat and tilts my face up to his. "I need your words, tiny dancer." He kisses the corner of my mouth before dragging my tongue between his and sucking.

And oh my God . . . nothing has ever lit my body up this way before.

"God, yes. *Please*, Ares. I need this." I hold his eyes for what feels like an eternity, but in reality, it's one single second frozen in time. It's one of those moments in life I know, with complete certainty, I'll never recover from. But I'd rather spend the rest of my life broken than wondering *what if*.

I've played it safe my entire life.

Done everything everyone has ever wanted.

I press my lips to his and hum deep in my throat before opening my eyes. "This is for me. This is what I want. *You're what I want.*"

His dark eyes close, and he inhales an intense, sexy breath.

"Do those words work for you?" I tease.

When he opens his eyes again, an inferno reflects back at me.

Guess they worked.

"Good girl," he growls.

My body vibrates under his touch. Strung so tightly, I'm ready to snap when his fingers slide along my panties. He teases me over the lace as his mouth trails down my neck with warm, wet kisses.

A needy, wanton moan slips past my lips.

I want more.

"Your skin is so fucking soft." His palm covers my sex, and heat pools in my belly with needy anticipation. "Open your eyes, Grace. Open those eyes and look at us. Look at how fucking hot you are."

His fingers push under the lace, and he hisses when they slide along my bare lips.

"So fucking hot and so fucking wet for me, baby."

I open my eyes and gasp because . . . *Wow* . . . He's right.

The reflection staring back at me is erotic and . . . beautiful.

His big body surrounds mine.

My legs shake as Ares teases me, not giving me what I want. But coming so damn close.

When he finally presses a finger inside me, my body clenches around him and practically purrs from the overwhelming sensation.

"Fucking drenched for me, my girl." He spins me around,

so my back is against the glass, and drags a hand down my ribs and flat to my stomach as he drops to his knees.

"What are you—"

I throw my head back and moan, longer and louder than I mean to, when he buries his face in the delicate lace of my panties. His tongue licks a line up along the lace, fanning the flames between us until they threaten to burn me alive.

"Ares," I beg and argue all at once, not sure if I want him to stop or start. "They can see . . . The people in the pod across from us . . . They can see us."

"Let them watch." He snaps my panties against my pussy before he slides the lace aside and flattens his tongue.

Oh, God.

He soothes one ache and creates another, and I forget anyone else even exists or if they can see us.

"Please," I beg. "I need . . . I need more."

And he does it again. *And again*. And again.

Stroking me. Tasting me. Growling against my skin until I'm writhing under his touch.

Desperate. Needy. Dying for more.

For him.

Ares pulls at the scraps of delicate lace on my hip bones and snaps them with his bare hands, ripping them from my body, and my eyes fly to his. It's the most deliciously sinful sight I've ever seen.

I gasp and bury my fingers in the hair curling under his dark hat, needing to ground myself. My body threatens to give out as my orgasm builds, powerful and intense. A tsunami, just out of reach but threatening destruction.

"For months, I've dreamed of your fucking taste, Grace. Of your body. Of what you'd sound like the first time you come on my tongue. I need you to give it to me, baby. Give me what I want."

I moan and shake and drag his face back to my throbbing clit.

"That's my girl," he practically growls against my pussy.

Those words . . . *Holy. Fuck.* They fan the red-hot flames threatening to incinerate the world around us until I can no longer speak or think or form words. I can only feel, and I feel fucking everything.

Ares Wilder is going to destroy me in one single night.

Fucking me with his tongue, and oh God, his fingers.

My juices coat his face, and those midnight blue eyes never leave mine.

I could come just like this.

He sucks my clit as I chase my orgasm, edging closer with each tease of his rough, calloused fingers inside my body.

My knees shake with every scrape of my walls.

I tremble with each stroke against my G-spot.

Like my body was made for his pleasure, and he plays it like the fucking athlete he is.

Teasing me, over *and over* and over.

Each high is higher than the last, then softer than the next. Edging me. Bringing me higher only to tease me again *and again*. Until my vision darkens, and I'm not sure I can take any more.

"Ares . . . *please*."

"Please what?" He smiles up at me.

I reach down and drag my thumb across his soaked lips, then suck it between my own. "Please make me come."

He growls against my pussy.

Growls.

And *oh God*, he scrapes his teeth over my throbbing clit, and I see literal stars.

They burst behind my eyes in a kaleidoscope of colors.

I shatter and shake on a silent scream as he works me through my orgasm, never letting up until he's wrung every last drop from my shuddering body. And when he rises and gently fixes my dress, his eyes never leaving mine and that sexy smile in place . . . that's when I know . . . I'm never going to get over Ares Wilder.

He's going to be my destruction.

But it's going to be a beautiful fall.

ARES

We ride back to Grace's flat in silence, not because we're uncomfortable, but instead because we're both hanging on by a fraying fucking thread. Her hand is in my lap, sandwiched between mine. Her head is on my shoulder, and her citrusy, vanilla scent has me ready to rip right out of my own skin.

I swear to God, if I thought there was any way to get away with it, I'd fuck her right here and now, in the back of this car, with absolutely not one single goddamned regret. Well . . . at least until someone saw Grace naked. Then I'd have to kill the fucker. So that, unfortunately, isn't an option.

A few minutes later, when the car pulls to a stop in front of her flat, we both scramble to get out of the backseat and up the damn steps as fast as humanly possible, weaving through the pub patrons on the sidewalk and ignoring the loud strains of the music that float through the hall.

We come to a messy stop in front of her door, unable to take our hands off each other. I slide her long hair over her bare shoulder, loving the way she squirms and sighs when I drag my lips down her neck while she tries, unsuccessfully, to unlock the door with trembling hands.

After her second try, she curses, and I chuckle. "You need help there, baby?"

A shiver skirts down her spine before her shoulders straighten, and she cocks her head over her shoulder, ready to reprimand me like a naughty librarian scolding a loudmouth.

Ohh . . . Naughty librarian. That could be fun.

"I need you to stop touching me and calling me *baby*, so I can think straight for thirty seconds, god of war."

I slide my hand inside the damn slit in her long dress—that had her incredible toned, tanned thigh playing peek-a-boo with me all day—and cup her sex before running a finger along the lips of her bare pussy.

"You really want me to stop touching you, Gracie?" I lick up her neck and around her ear lobe, loving how fucking responsive she is. I slide my hand along the soft, smooth skin of her thigh. "Now that I've had a taste of your sweet cunt, I'm never going to get enough. I need you laid out on your bed, baby. I need to take my time with you. I want to learn every fucking inch of your body. I want to know exactly how to make you scream. I want to know what you look like when you think you can't take any more. When you're begging for relief. I want to know what you feel like when you come on my cock."

"Ohmygod," she moans, and I slide two fingers deep inside her perfect pussy and curl them until I hit that spot that makes her fall forward against her door, shaking and moaning.

"Get the keys in the door, Grace, or I'm going to fuck you in this hall, and you're going to take every fucking inch of me and beg for more."

"How do you make filthy sound so fucking good?" She

backs her ass up into my dick, as frantically desperate for me as I am for her. With shaking hands, she tries to work the key one more time before finally opening the damn door, and we both practically fall inside.

I spin us around and press her back flat against the heavy wooden door, then link our fingers and hold both her arms hostage above her head. "Everything with you and me is going to be good, Grace. You'll see."

Her breasts press against my chest, and she bends a knee, wrapping it around my hip. "Fuck, Grace . . . You gonna show me just how flexible ballerinas are?"

Moonlight mixes with the streetlights outside and filters in through the curtains, giving her an almost iridescent glow. "I want to be the only ballerina you're thinking about," she taunts, and I brush my lips over hers.

"Only you, baby," I whisper against her lips and know with complete certainty I'll worship this woman with my dying breath.

Glassy, lust-filled eyes stare back at me as I claim her mouth.

Slowly. Savoring her soft lips and sweet, sexy little sighs.

I position both of her wrists in one of my hands and use the other to slide under her dress and cup the most perfect ass that ever existed.

Grace lifts both legs and locks them around my waist. Melting against me. Her delicate curves press against me. Soft where I'm hard and fucking flawless in my arms. This woman was made to be mine.

"We're going to take our time tonight. I'm going to worship you." I groan against her mouth, and she whimpers. The sound reverberates through me, and I know I'm as far gone as she is.

Drunk on her taste. Her sounds. Her smells.

I know without a single shadow of doubt, one night will never be enough.

Hell, one lifetime won't be enough.

"Ares." She tugs, trying to break free of my hold on her wrists. "I want to touch you."

My name on her lips might just be my new favorite sound.

I squeeze her bare ass, then smack it, and she moans into my mouth, breaking something that's been waiting, dormant, for her since that snowstorm months ago.

I'm *hungry* . . . Fucking ravenous. And Grace is the only thing to quiet that need.

She locks her long legs around my hips. Her heels dig into my ass, and she grinds her heated core against my hard cock. "Please," she pleads against my lips.

"Fuck, baby . . ." I let go of her wrists and wrap a hand around her throat, and those aqua eyes fly to mine, sparkling back at me.

She rocks her hips slowly with heavy eyes and runs her hands over my shoulders and down my shirt, clawing at the hem.

"I want to feel your skin," she pleads. Her hands slide under my shirt and press flat against my abs, searing my skin. Branding me. "Please, Ares. I need to feel you."

"You're gonna feel me for fucking days, baby." And just that thought has my cock growing harder. I need to be inside. Claiming her. *Mine* repeats over and over in my head, like a mantra in my mind.

"I want to feel you forever," she whispers, biting at my lower lip, then sucking it between hers.

Fuck . . . Does she even realize what she's saying?

I slide her off the door and adjust my hold, then cross the room and move into her bedroom. With a kick behind me, the door slams shut, and I lay my girl out on her bed. Her long, dark hair pools around her beautiful face, a stark contrast to her white comforter. The skinny straps of her soft, green sundress slip off her shoulders, and she brings her feet up flat on the bed, knees bent, with that damn thigh-high slit falling open and teasing me with the tiniest glimpse of her bare pussy.

She's a fucking vision. And she's mine.

"Take your hat and shirt off, god of war," she demands. "Let me see you."

I toss my hat to the side, then reach back and yank my shirt over my head, dropping it to the floor in time to see Gracie sit up and smile. And I know, in that moment, I'd do anything for that smile.

Kill for it.

Die for it.

"I knew you'd have a beautiful body," she whispers, then crawls on her knees to the edge of the bed and presses her hot mouth to the base of my jaw. "You are a work of art."

She drags her hand between us, her nails scraping down my bare chest, tracing each line of muscle before she lifts her molten eyes to mine. "A masterpiece," she whispers with an air of awe that gives me chills.

With deft fingers, she unbuckles my belt and jeans and hums a sexy little sound that I'll be dreaming of for the rest of my life when her hands slide inside and over my ass.

A tiny moan slips past her lips, and I know I'm a fucking goner. "Now it's my turn to get a taste."

"Baby, you have no idea how long I've dreamed about your mouth on me." I slide one of her minty-green, skinny straps off her arm, giving me a tantalizing tease of the swell of her breast. "But I need to fuck you before I lose my mind. And if your mouth is on me, I can't control when that happens."

A throaty laugh escapes her lips as she slips her arms out

of her dress and pulls it over her head, leaving her in absolutely nothing. *Nothing*. Grace sits back on her knees and peers up at me through long lashes, suddenly shy. "Ares . . ." she whispers, and *fuck me*. That tone is my undoing.

There isn't a single thing in this world I wouldn't do for this girl.

Wouldn't give to this girl.

Whether she realizes it yet or not, tonight is just the beginning.

I'm never giving her up.

I kick off my sneakers and shuck my jeans and boxers as Grace reaches for me.

Her hands hold my face as her nails skim the scruff on my jaw while she just stares at me. "I can't believe you're really here, and this isn't a dream," she whispers.

"We make our own reality, Grace. All you have to do is choose us."

And there goes that flush.

The one I love.

The one that kisses the tops of her cheeks and trails all the way down her chest.

Her breasts are perfect teardrops with pretty pink nipples, hard and taught and begging to be sucked. Long, lean dancer's muscles that are hard-earned and so damn sexy.

She's flawless.

"You're fucking perfect, Grace."

"Perfection isn't real. It's a game we play that ends with you disappointed later when the illusion cracks and the memory fades." Her face softens before she covers my mouth with hers. "I don't want *to have to be* perfect with you. I want you to see the real me."

She reaches down and takes my cock in her hand. "I've been numb for so long." Before I can ask her what she means, she strokes me once, then presses her tongue into my mouth. I have to fight the urge to flip her over and fuck us both into oblivion.

"I need to feel tonight, Ares." She kisses my chest. My abs. My lats. Then she looks up at me and licks her lips, so close to the tip of my cock. "Please . . . let me taste you."

She slides off the bed and onto her knees.

Her long lashes flutter, and her aqua eyes say so much more than her words.

"Grace . . ." I warn. I'm holding tightly to the last thin threads of restraint I've got left.

She tries to wrap her fist around my cock, and all the blood rushes from my body right to my dick before she presses a kiss to the tip.

Her tongue swirls the head, and she blinks up at me *innocently*, almost like she's asking for permission.

"You gonna be a good girl and suck my cock, baby?"

She freezes for a minute, unsure if she wants to like my words. But then those stunning fucking eyes sparkle and smile, and I'm done.

A white-hot, searing bolt of need builds from my spine and threatens to take me down. "Fuck, you look so pretty on your knees for me, Grace."

I run my thumb along her jaw until she opens her mouth and takes me on her tongue, licking me from base to tip.

I gather her soft hair in my hand and wrap it around my fist, tugging as her pretty pink lips stretch around my cock. Her eyes water, and she moans, adding her hand to my shaft and working me up and down.

She's a fucking sight to be seen, on her knees in front of me, taking me down her throat.

Naked.

Wet.

Wanting.

"Fuuuuck . . ." I growl when she swallows me down and slides her hand between her own legs, needing relief I can't wait to give her.

"No fucking way are you getting yourself off, Grace." I pull back, and she pouts so damn pretty. "You're mine, and I own your orgasms. You come when I say and how I say."

"I need to come now, Ares . . . Please. I want to feel your weight on my body. I need to feel you inside me."

I step back, and Grace frowns. "Where are you going?"

"Nothing in the goddamned world could keep me from fucking you right now, baby. I've just got to grab a condom from my bag."

She scoots onto the bed. One knee bent, one leg straight. Her head tilts my way, and the smile on her face . . . it takes my fucking breath away. "I've got an IUD. I had a physical before I started with the company. And I haven't been with anyone since then . . . I haven't been with anyone in a really long time . . ." The softness in her voice begs me to understand what she's telling me. "I'm clean . . ."

"I need your words, Grace." I reach for her and run my thumb over her cheek. "Because I'm clean too. We get physicals throughout the season. I've never been with anyone without a condom. And there's been no one else since you slept in my bed. Not a fucking woman in the world could hold a candle to you since that night. But I need you to be sure, baby."

"I don't want anything between us, Ares. I just want you." She reaches for me with a wicked gleam in her eye. "Don't treat me like glass, god of war. I'm not going to break."

Grace

A sliver of moonlight shining through the shades bathes the room in a cool, soft glow as Ares climbs on my bed, his body hovering over me. He's beautiful. Stacked muscles and colorful tattoos only add to the sexy package that is Ares Wilder.

He drags the thick head of his enormous cock through my sex. And of course, this man's dick is gigantic and might just split me in two. But oh, what a death it will be.

Ares teases me until I'm aching and trembling and begging for him.

I'm ready to scream, but when I open my mouth, deliciously calloused fingers wrap around my neck—the way he seems to enjoy doing—and my air is cut off just the tiniest fraction, and I'm at his mercy. Not thinking, just trusting him, and I do . . . I trust him in a way I've never trusted anyone else.

His mouth covers mine, and our tongues dance a wicked dance.

Each stroke of his tongue against mine heightens my need until I'm teetering on the edge of sanity, not sure how much more I can take but more than ready to find out.

I drape my arms around his shoulders and drag my nails down the planes of his back, digging into the thick muscle. Urging him on. Silently pleading for more.

Then when I wrap my legs around his waist and dig my heels into the globes of his ass, Ares finally, *finally*, pushes his cock deep inside me—filling me, overwhelming me, and owning me.

I gasp and moan. Agony and ecstasy battling for control.

Ares owns my mouth the same way he's owning my body.

Slowly. Sensually.

Until my muscles loosen and the painful stretch turns to scorching hot pleasure.

He inches in slowly before pulling back out.

Another inch each time.

Dragging against my sensitive walls.

Driving me insane.

Teasing me until I'm begging for more.

With each achingly slow stroke, his mouth worships mine.

Soothingly sexy words kiss my lips.

Until my muscles relax around him.

Stretching to take him deeper.

Clawing to get him impossibly closer.

Because I still need more . . . I need it all.

I want everything.

I'd give it all to him if I could.

One rough hand cups my face, holding me hostage while our tongues move in savage harmony. And when he finally thrusts all the way inside me until there's no space between us, I'm utterly consumed by him.

"Ares . . ."

His lips slip down the column of my neck, pressing against the hollow of my throat. His tongue licks a lazy circle. "Tell me how it feels, baby."

"I feel . . ." I gasp as he thrusts in again, so damn slowly, hitting that spot I never truly believed existed. "So fucking good. So fucking full." I gasp and then grasp at his ass, desperately willing him to move as I grind my hips against his. "I need . . . more," I moan as he licks and nips and drags his tongue down across my collarbones.

He pulls out slowly, then sucks one hard nipple into his mouth, and my back bows off the bed as Ares sets a punishing rhythm. With every hard thrust of his hips, his huge body dominates mine. Fucking me harder until I'm clinging to him, moaning and begging and worshipping at the altar of my own personal god.

His hands slide under me and grip my ass, holding me tightly against him.

Changing the angle and driving me insane.

"Tell me your mine, Grace." Ares's midnight eyes burn like a blue flame.

Intense and overwhelming and threatening to destroy us.

"I'm yours," I plead as I buck against him, and his mouth takes mine.

If only for tonight, I'm his . . .

Our connection is intense . . . insane . . . Threatening to burn out before it ever breathes.

It doesn't make sense, and yet somehow, it's the only *real* thing I have in my life.

"Baby . . ." Ares whispers, and I tighten around him.

My nails rake over his skin, and I scream out his name.

"Fuck, Grace . . ." Ares's lips capture mine, swallowing my moan as my vision goes black and my orgasm explodes.

A warm weight washes over me before he pulls out and paints my stomach with long ropey strands of his cum.

My name an almost silent benediction falling from his lips.

Ares gathers me in his arms and kisses the top of my hair.

As my eyes close, I become lost in his warmth and the restrained strength in his arms while I drift off to sleep. The word *mine* the only sound I hear. But is it my voice or his?

The Philly Press

KROYDON KRONICLES

HOCKEY HUNK IN HIDING

Have you seen Kroydon Hills's very own god of war lately? I have it on good authority that our favorite hockey hunk has left the country. But the bigger question we're all dying to know the answer to is, is he meeting someone there? Stay tuned because this reporter is living for all things.

#PuckPack #KroydonKronicles

GRACE

I pry my eyes open when the delicious smell of freshly brewed dark-roast coffee demands I wake up and not one minute before. Ares and I have spent the last few days in bed. My body hurts in ways I never realized would be possible, and I'm a professional dancer. That's saying something.

I throw on one of his t-shirts from the floor and rub my eyes, trying to clear the sleep as I wander into the living room to find Ares frying eggs in my kitchen. It's possibly the least-used room in the entire flat because Lennon and I are both slightly better than a five-year-old with their first Easy Bake Oven when it comes to cooking. We're much better at takeout and warming up leftovers.

But, *oh my* . . . If every day started with Ares Wilder standing in front of my stove in gray sweatpants and no shirt, I'd learn to appreciate the kitchen just a little bit more.

My mouth waters, but it's no longer from the smell of coffee.

Well, maybe just a smidge.

I walk up to him, wrap my arms around his waist, and

hum happily as he drops a kiss on my head. "Good morning," I murmur against his chest.

"Mornin', birthday girl." He flips the eggs over in the pan, then slides them onto two plates. "You hungry?"

I nod because words fail me as I stare at everything that is the man in front of me.

Two more days, and then he has to go home.

Two more days until our happy bubble bursts and reality comes crashing back down.

Two more days until I give him back.

But for now, I smile and grab both plates, along with the little pile of toast, and take them over to the table, then turn and watch my own personal Greek god add cream to my coffee just the way I like it and carry both mugs over. "So . . . Jenkins messaged . . ."

"Jenkins . . ." Ares thinks about it for a minute. "The director?"

"Yup. He asked if I'd stop by the studio today to work on choreography for the audition next week." I sip my coffee and enjoy the view because it is spectacular and rivals any I've ever seen. "Any chance you'd want to come watch? We could grab dinner after."

Ares scoops me up and sits me down in his lap. "You telling me I get to watch you dance again?"

I slide one leg over his lap and straddle his strong thighs. "You don't mind?"

He wraps one big hand around the back of my neck and digs his fingers into my tight muscles. "No, baby. I don't mind. How about I show you just how much I don't mind . . ."

My phone rings with my sister's ringtone, and I jump up. "Shit. I didn't call Evie."

I run to grab it from the bedroom and wince when my foot screams in pain. *Fuck.*

"You just woke up," Ares laughs behind me. "What the hell is she even doing awake?"

"Shh." I wave him away and answer her FaceTime, "Happy Birthday, sissy."

Her face pops up with a sleeping one-year-old Jax resting on her chest. "Happy birthday, sissy," she whispers back. "I wanted to be the first to say it."

Ares laughs, and I kick him as Everly's face scrunches.

"Was that Lennon? I thought she was going home this week?"

I walk away from Ares, hiding my limp. I've definitely overdone it the past few days. "No. It wasn't Lennon. It wasn't anybody. What are you doing up with Jax at three a.m.?"

Everly presses a kiss to Jax's head. "He spiked a fever earlier and only wants to sleep if he's on me. Funny to think I met his daddy exactly one year ago today."

"First birthday we ever spent apart," I muse. "Guess the universe decided to reward you with Cross Wilder. Not a bad trade-off."

"Yeah," she hums quietly with a contented smile. "Best reward I could have ever dreamed of. But I still wish we weren't spending our birthday apart two years in a row. Are you doing anything special today?"

I look over at Ares, standing on the other side of the room with his arms crossed over his delectable chest.

"Nothing *too* special." I flinch as the words choke me like dry sawdust in my mouth. "I heard Mom is throwing you a dinner tonight. I wish I was going to be there."

Everly doesn't bother hiding the hurt. "You could have been here. But you'd rather be home *alone* than at the beach with your family."

"Evie . . . you're going to have to stop the guilt trips. I'm meeting with Jenkins today to go over audition choreography. I needed to stay here."

"I'm sorry. I just miss you." Her frustration quickly morphs, and I recognize the concerned look in her eyes. "I thought you were taking off and taking it easy this week. How's your foot? Are you resting it? Did you have your follow-up yet?"

"Yes, *mom*. I'm taking it easy," I assure her as Ares eyes burn into the back of my head.

"Don't give me that shit. You haven't even told Mom you're hurt."

"I haven't said anything because she'd worry. I'm fine," I insist, as I move through my bedroom into my bathroom and sit on my counter. "A few days off is all I needed."

Nothing like hiding in your own flat.

Shit.

"How's everyone back home?" I change the subject and turn the shower on. "How are the boys?"

"Well, I told you Nixon moved in with Ares. But did you hear that now Bellamy and Caitlin live there too? Ares is probably fucking Caitlin. Who knows? But Sam will kill him if he finds out. Maddox too, so there's that."

Even knowing that's not happening, the idea that another woman gets to see him every day hurts like hell.

Another reason why this can't possibly work.

Long distance would be bad by itself, but add in our careers, and it's a recipe for disaster.

"Nix is super excited to be staying in Kroydon Hills. Cross and Easton and Ares have been practicing with him already. Not sure Dad has come to grips with the fact his son is playing pro hockey instead of football, but he's trying. Leo and Henny stayed on campus in the hockey house at the college for the summer. Mom wasn't thrilled, so she's hyperfocusing on Jax and Kerrigan. My kids are a whole new level of spoiled that even we weren't. But truthfully, I'm not trying to guilt you. I think she just misses having us all home."

My heart pangs.

I miss being home.

"Uncle Tommy went fishing with Cross and Kerrigan and Ares last week, and the four of them were so excited they caught a big fish. Then Kerrigan lost her mind when they told her they were going to cook it. She made Uncle Tommy take it off the hook and throw it back into the lake. Now she wants a pretty pet fish—not eating fish. *Her exact words.*"

I lean back against my mirror and force a sad smile.

I'm missing it.

All of it.

"Aww. Are you guys going to get her a fish?" I ask, remembering how quickly our fish used to die and how hard we'd cry each time.

"No," Everly laughs softly. "Ares promised her he would. Kerrigan has all her uncles wrapped around her tiny little fingers."

Jax opens his eyes and lets out a pained cry. "Shit." Everly drops the phone, then quickly bends to pick it up. "Gotta go, sissy. Love you."

"Love you too, Evie. Tell everyone hi for me."

"Come home and tell them yourself," she challenges with a smile. "Fine. I'll tell them."

Everly ends the call, and tears well in my eyes.

The floor creaks, and I turn to find Ares standing in the door. "I'm not fucking Caitlin." His voice has an angry edge I've never heard from him before.

I wipe my eyes and gingerly jump down off the counter, then adjust the temperature of the shower. "I know."

"Any reason you lied to your sister?"

"I didn't lie. My foot is fine. It really hasn't been bothering me much this week."

A strange look comes over his face, and I realize that wasn't what he was talking about as he crowds me, forcing me back, then plants his palms flat against the wall on either side of my face. "Why didn't you say anything if it was bothering you?"

"Because I'm a professional, and I'm fine." I cup his scruff-covered jaw in my hands. "I have a very high pain tolerance." Steam billows out of the shower and wraps around us. "You want to take a shower with me?"

Ares steps back out of my hold. "I'm going to go clean up breakfast." He kisses my forehead and leaves the room and me in it, wondering what the hell just happened.

Ares

NIXON

Dude. When are you coming home?

ARES

I'm on a red-eye tomorrow night.

Why? You didn't burn my place down, did you?

BELLAMY

Hey. We're all adults. We can handle a few days without you.

ARES

If you have to announce you're an adult, I should probably be worried.

CAITLIN

No, shithead. Nothing has burned down. Nothing has broken. And only one skank has been thrown out. Your boyfriend just misses you.

NIXON

Don't be a bitch, Cait. I'm just tired of being outnumbered.

And she wasn't a skank.

CAITLIN

Sure she wasn't.

ARES

I thought you were all at the beach.

BELLAMY

Heading down this afternoon.

NIXON

Yeah. I'm driving.

BELLAMY

You offered.

CAITLIN

I can drive.

BELLAMY

NO.

NIXON

NO.

ARES

How many cars have you crashed this year?

CAITLIN

This year? Only two.

NIXON

Only . . . Only, she says.

ARES

> Don't burn my house down.

I close out of my messages and drop down on the edge of Grace's bed, wondering how today went sideways so quickly.

"Hey," she whispers a few minutes later, and I look up.

Grace walks over to me, freshly showered and wrapped in a fluffy, white towel. Her long, dark hair is piled high on her head with damp tendrils framing her face. So much warm, pink, soft skin.

She moves between my legs and takes my phone out of my hands, then tosses it to the nightstand.

I wrap my hands around the backs of her long legs and drop my head to her chest.

Grace's fingers dig into my hair, massaging my scalp. "Why were you angry earlier?"

I run my hands up the back of her bare legs under her towel and drag her closer. "I don't want to do this today. It's your birthday."

"Do what?" I look up and watch her eyes flick over my face, searching.

She's going to force my hand.

Son. Of. A. Bitch.

"Ares . . ." She holds the knot in her towel tightly and straddles my lap. "What are you talking about?"

My hands move to her back, holding her in place. "Why'd you lie to your sister?"

"I told you, I didn't lie," she argues in a sugary sweet voice.

The swells of her breasts rise and fall with each deep breath, and I swear to fucking God, the last thing I want to do is fight with her. "Gracie . . ."

"What? I didn't lie."

"I saw the pills on your counter."

Her face pales. "You're not— I didn't mean—"

"You told me you were fine, good twin. Told your sister the same thing."

She bites down on her bottom lip and looks away, like she's searching for the answer. "It's not like that."

"Not like what, Grace?" I wait for an answer, but she refuses to look at me. "If you're fine, why did you pop an Oxy?"

Fuck. I know I'm being a dick.

But. She. Lied.

You don't lie if you've got everything under control.

"I was going to take this week. I was supposed to rest . . . I'll stay off it today and be fine tomorrow." She finally gives me her eyes, and pain is swirling behind her pretty blues.

"How long has it been since you saw the doctor?" I push.

"What?" Grace plays dumb. Something she definitely isn't, so my girl is avoiding like a champ.

"You have a prescription in your bathroom. You must have seen a doctor. When did you see them?" I move toward the bathroom, and she blocks me.

"Excuse me?"

Oh, yeah. Now that pain is replaced by fire.

She's pissed. Good. Let her be mad.

"When did you see the damn doctor, Grace? What did they say was wrong?" I bend my knees and cradle her face in my hands. "And don't tell me it's nothing. You wouldn't need Oxy if it was nothing."

She tries to shove me away, but I don't let go. "Who the hell do you think you are, Ares Wilder?"

"I'm the man who's in love with you, Grace."

She gasps at my admission, then closes her mouth and shakes her head. "You're not. You like the idea of me. We've spent three days together. You don't even know me."

"If you believe that, you're lying to your sister and yourself."

I reach into my bag and pull out the gift-wrapped box and toss it to her.

"What's this?" she asks as she catches the robin's-egg blue box with the giant white bow.

"Your birthday present. I need to get out of here."

"Ares," she calls after me, but I'm already gone.

I've done this before.

I'm not doing it again.

GRACE

I watch him walk through the door, and my stomach drops.

My hands shake, and my legs give out as I slide down against my bed until my ass hits the floor. *He just left.* He told me he was in love with me, then left. *What?*

I didn't mean—

I'm not sure how . . .

Oh my God.

My phone rings in the bathroom, but I don't get up. I can't. I'm not sure my legs would hold me if I even tried to. *What have I done?*

I replay our fight over in my mind, and guilt claws at me.

I close my eyes and press my cheek against my knees as the first tear falls and a sob rips from my throat. Then I'm lifted in strong arms and pulled onto Ares's lap like the most precious thing in the world. "I thought you left," I cry.

"Yeah well, I was going to. But you don't leave when you've got something worth fighting for. And you're worth everything, Grace. But you've got to be honest with me. That's the only way this works. I can't stand liars."

"The truth?" I ask, laughing through my tears. "I'm not even sure what that is anymore."

"How about we start with why you're numb?" he counters as his hold on me tightens. "The other night you told me you're numb, and you just wanted to feel something. Why are you numb, baby? Is it from the pain or something else?"

The dam inside me breaks, and a gut wrenching sob rips from my throat. I cry uncontrollably until I can't breathe or think or remember why I'm fighting so damn hard to stay here. I cling to Ares and ugly cry until my throat hurts and my face is bright red and soaked with tears. Until I've drenched his shirt, and I still can't stop.

Ares holds me through it all.

He runs his hands over my hair soothingly, whispering over and over, "It's okay. Whatever it is, we can get through it. Let it out, baby. Let it all out. I've got you."

I have absolutely no idea how much time has passed before the sobs stop.

My throat is raw, and my eyes are dry and heavy when I finally lift my face to his, scared to death of the judgment I'm going to see shining back.

Only I don't . . . There's no judgment. Just concern.

"I hate my life," I admit so quietly I'm not sure I even said it.

"Then let's change it," he answers right away. Like it's the most obvious thing in the world.

"What?"

"If you're unhappy, let's figure out what's causing it and fix it. You shouldn't have to resort to drugs to get through your days, Grace."

"I'm not. I swear." I press my lips together and shake my head. "I have previously undiagnosed stress fractures of the second and third metatarsal bones that never healed properly. That's what the script is for. But if you look at the bottle, it's nearly three months old, and I have over half of them left. I swear I really do take them sparingly. I promise you, I don't have a problem. Or at least I wouldn't if I wasn't a dancer."

"How long would you need to sit out to heal?" he asks very carefully. Like I'm a baby deer he's expecting to bolt at any moment.

He's not wrong. Because I've never had this conversation with anyone.

And I don't know if I can have it now.

My phone rings in the bathroom again.

"Ignore it," Ares tells me, and I flinch. Because I have no doubt it's Jenkins, and the idea of disappointing him is almost worse than the idea of losing Ares.

"It's probably my director," I admit softly. "I need to answer it."

Ares's grip tightens, and a muscle ticks in his jaw. "Does your director know you're hurt?"

I nod. "The company doctor did my MRIs and wrote the script. We sign a contract that he can share any necessary medical information with the company. Jenkins knows everything."

"How long, Grace?" When I don't answer, he practically vibrates with anger. "How long has your director known you were hurting yourself, and how long do you have to rest for your foot and heal to dance without pain?"

"At least eight weeks. That's half the cycle of a show," I answer softly because saying it out loud is terrifying. "Four weeks practice. Three months production. One week off before we lather, rinse, and repeat. But even then, I may never dance without some pain."

"Can you take a show off? Will your spot still be there when you come back?"

I laugh a silent laugh.

"Hypothetically . . . yes. Will I ever make it back to principal dancer? Probably not. I don't think Jenkins would ever let me dance for him again either, if I leave now." I turn in his arms and cup his face in my hands. "And he has a lot of pull in my world. One phone call could kill any hope of ever reviving my career if I leave now."

"You said you hated your life, baby. Maybe it's time we switch up *your* world."

"It's the only thing I've ever known. It's what makes me, me . . ."

"It's your birthday . . . Maybe it's time to reinvent yourself."

"I wouldn't even know where to begin to do that." I rest my forehead against his.

"We'll figure it out." And it's the *we* that might actually destroy me most.

"Will you hold my hand?" I beg, trembling.

"Every step of the way." He presses his lips to mine, and I hang on for dear life because I'm about to throw everything I've worked so hard for into the fire and watch it burn. Whether I'll manage to walk through the flames has yet to be seen.

The Philly Press

KROYDON KRONICLES

SAY IT AIN'T SO

Do you believe in coincidences? Just spotted leaving the Philadelphia airport is none other than the god of war himself and a mystery brunette. It was hard to see who, but don't worry, this reporter loves a good challenge.

#PuckPack #KroydonKronicles #ChallengeAccepted

ARES

Grace is practically crawling out of her skin when we get to Heathrow Airport the next morning. We spent the majority of her birthday, yesterday, lining things up to take the next three months off. Step one is going home.

"I need you to tell me I'm doing the right thing," she whispers, once we take our seats for our six a.m. flight back to Philadelphia. "Tell me I didn't just blow up my career."

"Sixteen weeks, baby. Sixteen weeks to rest and rehab and come back bigger and badder than before."

Her body shakes with quiet laughter, and I wish I could bottle the sound.

My girl cried enough yesterday to last a lifetime, and I wanted to kill that fucking director of hers for the way he made it worse. He might as well have told her if she took the time off, she'd never come back to his company as a principal dancer. But Grace still agreed this was what she needed.

"Ballerina, Ares." She pulls me out of my raging thoughts. "Not hockey player. Bigger isn't better."

"You sure about not telling anyone you're coming home?"

I press her, and she lifts her head and smiles a nervous little smile.

"Not even a little bit." She closes her eyes and rests her head on my shoulder. "This is going to be such a clusterfuck."

"With your overinvolved family and friends . . . *What*? You think they're all going to have an opinion?"

She smacks my chest and laughs a little louder this time, then happily accepts the blanket the flight attendant offers and lifts the arm rest between us. "Shut up, god of war. They're your family and friends now too."

"They are. But the difference is I don't give a shit what any of them think of me." I've never been the guy who cares what other people think. But that's not my girl. She cares about everything and everyone. She wears her heart on her sleeve and is pure as fucking snow. That's why everyone always wants to protect Grace.

"You gonna teach me that fancy trick? The not-caring thing?"

"I am, baby. Because as much as I want to stand up for you, I want you to be able to stand up for yourself even more." I kiss the top of her head and relax as the plane takes off.

"And you're really not going to be mad if we keep us quiet and low-key for now?"

Yeah . . . That's the other reason I need my girl not to give a flying fuck what anybody thinks about her. *Because she's not ready to share us with everyone else . . . Not yet.*

Her words. Not mine.

But if that's what she needs, that's what I'm gonna give her.

She doesn't need me making things harder right now.

"Yeah, baby. We'll make it work," I promise, even if I fucking hate this idea.

"One step at a time," she agrees. "Let me get through this nightmare first."

"You're stronger than you think, Grace."

"Guess we're going to find out."

After eight hours on a plane, an hour waiting for our luggage, and another hour and a half driving down to the tiny shore town Grace's family might as well own, so many of them have houses here, we finally pull up in front of Cross and Everly's beachfront house. But once the ignition is off, Gracie doesn't move to get out of the truck.

"I'm not sure I can do this." Her frightened eyes dance between the house and me. "What if we just go back to Kroydon Hills and lie low until everyone comes home from the beach in a few days?"

I move around the truck then and open her door.

She turns toward me and spreads her legs for me to stand between them, then circles her arms around my neck. "I hate this."

"There's nothing to hate. Your family is just going to be happy your home." I press my lips to hers and pull her chest against mine, knowing this might be the last time I get to do this for a while. "Come on, tiny dancer. You got this."

"I'd rather have you," she murmurs against my lips.

"Say the word, baby. All you've got to do is say the word, and I'll tell the world you're mine." Fuck . . . that's what I wish she'd do.

"No . . . One thing at a time. You're right. Time to face the music."

Grace

Ares and I walk up to Cross and Everly's place and knock on the massive front door before letting ourselves in. *She's my twin.* We don't really *do* privacy.

"Hello," I call out and follow the sound of little-girl giggles coming our way. My niece, Kerrigan, runs by us, then skids to a halt in a lime-green polka-dot bikini with matching ribbons in her space buns and screams before launching herself at Ares. "Uncle Ares is here, Daddy."

Her incredible hot uncle catches her and tosses her high in the air above his head until her giggles are deafening. *And holy shit*. I think my eardrums may have just burst, that was so high-pitched with excitement.

When she looks over his shoulder and sees me, she screams again. "And so is Aunt Gracie."

"What?" Cross groans and walks into the room, looking exhausted and covered in . . . *flour*? "Good, you're here," he grumbles, then looks between his brother and me. "What the hell?"

"Hi." I wave, and he wraps an arm around me. "Does your sister know you're coming? Evie . . ." he calls out, then looks between us again. "What are you doing here? And why are you together?"

"We bumped into each other at the airport," I lie. The first of many I'll be telling for a while and suddenly realize Ares is right.

I'm a liar.

And I'm making him one too.

"What the heck is going on in here?" Everly asks as she

walks into the room with Jax clinging to her. "Ohmygod, Gracie... *Ohmygod.*"

She passes her son off to Cross and grabs me so hard, I think she might actually leave a bruise.

"Hi," I laugh and pat her back. "Surprise."

"Best surprise ever," she squeals, and I now understand where Kerrigan gets the ear-piercing sound from. "I can't believe you're here. I thought you couldn't come. How long are you home for? How did you get here?" Then she looks between me and Ares. "And why are you here with him?"

"Slow down and let her breathe, blondie," Ares laughs.

Oh shit. The death stare she gives Ares could make a lesser man run for his life. But not Ares. He laughs at her. "Calm down, Everly. I ran into Ares at the airport and hitched a ride. I wanted to surprise you."

Okay. Not a complete lie.

"I can't believe you're here." She steps back and holds my arms out to look at me. "Shit, Grace. Did you lose more weight? Come on. We just made pancakes. Eat something."

"Daddy made chocolate-chip pancakes cause he said they make Mommy nicer," Kerrigan tells us matter-of-factly. "I helped cut up the strawberries."

Ares kisses the top of her head, then puts her down and takes her hand in his. "Sounds like we got here just in time. Lead the way, princess."

Kerrigan beams, and my ovaries ache.

Sexy Ares is so fine, but Uncle Ares... well he's just a whole other level of hot.

And he's mine.

We walk into the kitchen, where it looks like more flour made it onto the floor than in a bowl. Everly pours her and me coffee and makes me a plate of pancakes like I'm one of her kids. "Come on. Let's sit outside. I want to hear everything."

I follow her onto her porch and steal the maple syrup off the table as I go. "I just talked to you yesterday. Not much has changed since then."

Lie number two.

Everything's changed.

"Bullshit. You're here instead of telling me to back off." She sips her coffee and steals a strawberry off my plate. "Now spill it, sissy."

"Okay, but you've got to let me deal with Mom and Dad."

Her face falls. "Oh shit. You're pregnant. Fuck, Grace. Please tell me Ares is not the father and that's not why you got here together. I'll kill him."

"Bite your tongue. I'm not pregnant," I snap and throw a strawberry at her face. At least that's not a lie. "I'm taking a few weeks off to rehab my foot. If I don't do it now, it won't ever heal properly. I'm going to see if Brynlee will work with me."

"A few weeks? I didn't realize it was that bad."

She didn't realize because I didn't tell her.

"Yeah . . . I'm going to sit out this next show cycle. I'm scared if I don't, I'll never dance again."

"Gracie . . ." She grabs my hand and squeezes. "You can't not dance. You were born for it."

I don't bother correcting her.

I don't tell her I'm not sure if I even want to dance anymore.

I don't tell her how miserable I've been or how much I've hated these past few months.

I just rest my hand on hers and smile.

"What time are we meeting everyone at the beach?"

GRACE

My family is full of traditions.

Sundays are sacred, and our church is a football stadium. Thanks to my brothers and brother-in-law, they're shared with hockey these days. But football will always come first.

Thanksgiving dinner is always at Grandpa's house, even if that means the family—*The entire family*— has to celebrate it on a different day. Nearly thirty of us all. It wasn't always easy, considering Dad and two of my four uncles played pro football and Grandpa coached. Still does. Uncle Tommy has been his assistant for years, and now Dad's a quarterback coach.

Christmas means *The Nutcracker* ballet. First performed by Mom's baby ballerinas, then going into the city to see it or be in it.

And our entire family gets together for one week every July to celebrate birthdays at our beach compound. As a kid, this week was my favorite. Callen is only a week older than Everly and me. And yes, our family dynamic is a little strange because he's also technically our uncle. The three of us have celebrated our birthdays together most of our lives. Last year was the first year we missed it.

I was touring the country with an amazing company, performing *Giselle*. Everly was working. And well, Callen . . . he was preoccupied with one of his many girlfriends. Not that you can really call them girlfriends if you don't know their last names. And he never knows their last names. I'm not even sure he knows their first names half the time.

But it's the one time each year that all the Sinclairs, Murphys, and Ryans come together for a few days to relax and have fun. And I can't believe I was going to skip it. Especially right now as I sit, surrounded by my sister, cousins, and a few of our closest friends with our chairs in the sand and our toes in the warm ocean waves, watching the boys toss a football around.

Brynlee is on one side of me while Everly is on the other. And neither has stopped talking since we drug our chairs down to the water's edge. I push my glasses up into my hair and turn to Brynn. "Are you sure you don't mind if I stay with you for a few weeks? I'm sure I could always crash with Mom and Dad if I need to."

"I told you, *we* have room," Everly answers first, and Brynn laughs and smacks my leg with her paperback.

"Don't be stupid. I've got more than enough room. It's a five bedroom, and I'm only using one room, now that Kenzie's in DC for her residency."

Bellamy and Caitlin lean forward in their chairs. "Are you looking for roommates? I mean, I love living with Ares, but having my own room wouldn't be terrible."

"Hey," Cait bitches. "At least I don't snore."

"I do not snore."

"How long do you think you're going to be home, Grace?" Brynn ignores everyone else.

"I'm not sure. At least two months. I've got to see how

everything goes. Jenkins was furious when I told him I was taking time off to heal. I'm not sure if he's going to let me come back." I think back to how pissed he was when I bailed on him yesterday. "I think I'll be more surprised if he does let me come back, to be honest."

"What are you going to do if he doesn't?" my cousin Lilah leans forward and asks with a giant smile. She's a few years younger than Everly and me, but she's been touring the world for a few years. First as an opening act for a popular boy band, and now, as the main event on the ticket. I'm in complete awe of her world domination. "I could use a new choreographer."

"Grace isn't going to give up ballet," Everly answers for me, and I don't correct her.

"What was wrong with your last choreographer?" I ask instead.

"She refuses to see that I'm not the sixteen-year-old trying to market to the tween-age set anymore. If I want to be taken seriously, I've got to be allowed to grow as an artist. This album we're working on now is the first time I've really been in love with what I'm doing. It's supposed to wrap by the end of the summer, and the tour kicks off this fall."

A football lands at our feet, and I look up to find Ares jogging our way with a one-year-old Jax on his hip. Red board shorts hug his lean hips, stretched over thick thighs, and I slide my mirrored sunglasses back in place so I can stare properly without getting caught. I'd dare anyone to not stare at that man holding a baby. It's impossible.

Can you feel your ovaries exploding?

Because I think mine just did.

Lilah picks the ball up and hands it to Jax, who hides his face against Ares's chest. And the smile he gives my popstar cousin may or may not make my eye twitch the tiniest bit.

Brynn elbows me gently.

Shit. Was I that obvious?

She's the only person who has any clue what happened after Everly's wedding or that Ares and I have been talking since. Even if I haven't had a chance to fill her in on everything that's happened this week.

She's going to lose her mind.

"Ladies," Ares laughs as Jax continues to hide.

Everly stands and tries to take her baby from her brother-in-law, but Jax refuses to budge.

Can't blame you, kid. If I was wrapped around that naked chest, I'd refuse to move too.

"Damn . . . You Wilders are so hot," Lilah laughs at Bellamy, who just shakes her head.

"Ehh. They're okay." Bellamy sips her water but keeps her eyes focused on the guys in the ocean. My brothers are out there with Callen and Maddox and a few of our cousins. And I guess I'd feel the same way if someone told me Nixon, Leo, or Henny were hot. Even just thinking it gives me the icks.

I mean, I know they're handsome. But that's as far as I want to go.

Ares puts Jax down, and his little orange bucket hat slides sideways as he runs to Bellamy. "BB," he calls out for her before he trips into her open arms. "Go in the ocean wif me, BB."

He doesn't even know who I am.

To him, I'm a face on a phone or a computer.

And that hurts my heart.

Bellamy stands and takes Jax's hand. "I'm going to take Jax in the ocean, okay, Everly?"

My sister smiles, and I decide I want in on the auntie love. "Hold up. You've been the favorite aunt his whole life. Share the wealth," I joke and take Jax's other hand.

"Maybe you should move back home permanently," Everly calls out.

I'm starting to think maybe she's right.

Ares

"So, you and Gracie just happened to be at the airport together?" Grace's dad, Declan, asks me as he hands me a sandwich later that afternoon. Luckily, he doesn't wait for an answer. "I'm sure she appreciated that convenient coincidence."

"I was happy to be there." I don't elaborate. I like Declan. He's a good guy, and he accepted Cross and our whole family as part of his own immediately. I don't like the idea of lying to him. But I promised Grace we'd keep things quiet for now.

"She seems happy today," he muses, staring out into the ocean where the girls are standing, cooling off. "Not sure she's been that happy lately."

Alarm bells go off in my head.

I've got to tread carefully here.

"I'm sure she'll feel better once she rehabs." There. That was a safe answer.

Declan crosses his thick arms over his chest. The man might be in his late forties, but he was still the number-one pro quarterback in the country just a few years ago. He's just as jacked now as he was in his prime.

"Yeah," he draws out quietly. "I think so too. Not sure I'll be ready for her to go back to London after having her home for a few weeks though."

That makes two of us, but I can't tell him that.

Declan reaches into the cooler and pulls out two beers. He hands me one, then stares off into the ocean again. "Did anybody tell you the story of my brother, Cooper, and his wife?"

"Carys? The one who owns the lingerie shop?" I ask, pretty sure I'm right. Their family is huge, and it takes some getting used to when you grew up without any cousins or grandparents.

"Yeah. They spent a year together before they let anyone know."

And I choke on my beer.

"Crazy, right? Why would anyone hide being happy from their family? But Carys had it in her brain that she wasn't ready for anyone to know. And as men, we go along with what they want. I know I did. At least that's what Belles thought when it was us. She wanted to keep me in the friend zone, so I had to take my time and break down her walls. I had to show her we were worth it. In a way, I think that's what Coop had to do too."

Now it's my turn to stare out at the girls because there's no way in hell I'm looking Declan Sinclair in the eyes and lying to his face.

"It worked out in the long run for both of us. But it takes a certain kind of man with a certain level of confidence and patience to do that. Rushing a woman never works. And lord knows, my girls are stubborn just like their mother. I was glad Everly found Cross. He's a good man. You're a good man too, Ares. Not sure you think that though. But trust me. I'm a great fucking judge of character."

He smacks me on the back. "Good talk."

I have no clue how the hell I'm supposed to respond to any of this.

"Yeah, Dec. Good talk," I agree because what the hell am I supposed to say?

"Might want to get out there though. Looks like those

guys who were talking to Callen earlier are hitting on the girls."

I look back to the ocean and groan.

Dumb fucks.

When I turn back to Declan, he's laughing.

"For future argument's sake, I never said anything today," I grunt.

"Not a word, Wilder." Declan laughs at me as I jog out to where Maddox, Nixon, and Callen are standing near the girls.

"Who are the douchebags?" I growl.

Maddox laughs at me. "Way to be strangely overprotective of your sister, man."

"Yeah well, have *your* sister spend half her life in a hospital and see what it does to you," I answer honestly. Even if that's not at all why I'm pissed. Cross and I are protective of Bellamy, but if we tried to tell her who she could and couldn't date, she'd skin us alive.

"Listen, just because Cait would slice anyone who fucks with her into tiny little pieces doesn't mean all the girls are like that." Callen grabs the ball out of Nixon's hands and nods at me. "Go long, Wilder."

I go long for the pass.

The one that's going right at the girls.

Then I laugh out fucking loud when Callen, the tight end for the Philadelphia Kings, *accidentally* hits the dude closest to Grace in the head.

Fuck. I knew I liked him.

The girls jump back, and the douchebag whines like a bitch when I pick up the ball.

"Oopsie. Sorry, man," Callen tells the group of them once he's moved in front of the girls. "Guess that's why I'm not the quarterback."

Oopsie?

I fucking die.

Oopsie. I couldn't make this shit up.

And when Grace looks at me with a small smile as she giggles, I want to high-five Callen and tell him I owe him one.

GRACE

"How are you doing, sweetheart?" Mom sits down on the blanket next to me and digs her toes in the sand. Anabelle Sinclair is the woman I've always strived to be. She was a professional ballerina at the height of her career when her parents died and designated her as guardian of our Uncle Tommy. Mom gave it all up—*everything*—the career she loved, the life she'd worked so hard for—to come back to Kroydon Hills and keep what was left of her family together. And according to her, she has no regrets.

Uncle Tommy still lives with Mom and Dad. He has autism and needs a little extra help with some things, but he's basically my favorite person in the world. According to Dad, he was also clutch in convincing Mom to date Dad.

Thanks, Uncle Tommy.

Mom gave me my first pair of ballet shoes.

She helped me sew on the laces of my first pointe shoes years later.

She introduced Everly and me to every form of dance there was to learn and let us join every single one of the dance classes she offered at Hart & Soul, the studio she owns in Kroydon Hills. She was also the first person to tell me I'd outgrown what she could teach me when I was a sophomore in high school and encourage me to spread my wings. She's the person I've never wanted to let down, and she's looking at me right now with pity in her eyes that's making my stomach roll.

"You spent a lot of time on your feet on uneven sand today. You doing okay?"

She's also the biggest momma bear ever, and she worries about everything.

"I'm fine, Mom." I wrap my arms around my knees and relax. "Just felt like watching the sun set."

"Are you staying down here for the rest of the week?" She links her arm through mine and leans against me as we watch my uncles surfing in the distance.

"I think so. Everly said I could stay with Cross and her while I'm here, and Brynn said I could stay with her once we're back in Kroydon Hills." I catch Kerrigan out of the corner of my eye, running down the beach with a kite behind her.

"You know there's always room at our house. Daddy and I are going back to Kroydon Hills tonight. He's probably waiting for me."

"I know." I lean my head against hers. "But the boys are staying with you. At least the babies at Everly's are babies."

"Very true," she giggles as we watch Uncle Cooper wipe out.

"I'll be back in Kroydon Hills this weekend. I promise." I still can't believe I'm here.

It's my favorite time of night here. The sky is a watercolor painting of pinks and purples as the sun dips down behind the dark ocean. The vacationers have packed it up for the day and gone back to the houses, and I get my own little slice of heaven to myself.

It's calm. *Peaceful.* I missed peace.

"You want to tell me why you forgot to mention you were hurt?" Mom's voice is quiet but firm. She's hurt I kept it from her, but she's upset too.

"I didn't want you to worry. I had it under control. I just needed to finish the show and decide if I was good enough to jump right into the next one or not." In theory, that sounds believable. Even if it's not exactly how it happened.

"You have to take care of yourself. I taught you to listen to your body, Gracie."

"And I did, Mom. I saw the company's doctor. I took care of myself during the run of the show and came home to rehab now that it's over." Every time another lie leaves my lips, they get a little easier.

"You'd tell me if it was worse than you're letting on, wouldn't you? We could get a second opinion—"

"Mom," I stop her. "I'm okay. I've got this. I promise."

She gives me a look that I'm pretty sure means she's not sure whether to believe me or not. She runs her hand over my head, then kisses my cheek. "I love you, Gracie girl."

"Love you too, Mom. I'll stop by once I get settled in the condo this weekend."

"You better." She stands and wipes the sand off her jeans shorts.

My phone vibrates as she walks away, and my heart skips a beat when I see Ares's name pop up.

ARES

I want to peel that damn bikini off your body with my teeth.

GRACE

Hmm . . . I'd probably have to stay in a sandy bikini until everyone goes to bed tonight.

ARES

We're going to have to get creative.

GRACE

I like the sound of that.

The phone vibrates again, and this time, it's my sister.

EVERLY

Dinner at my house tonight. Let's surprise Gracie.

NIXON

Are you cooking?

EVERLY

Fuck no. I already ordered from Steve & Cookies. It should be here in an hour.

LEO

I'm in.

HENDRIX

Can I bring my laundry?

EVERLY

Sure. But I'm not Mom. You know where to find the washer and dryer. You're a big boy. You can do it yourself.

LEO

I wouldn't be so sure about that . . .

HENDRIX

Fuck off, asshole. I thought it was fabric softener.

NIXON

First problem with that statement - what grown ass man uses fabric softener?

EVERLY

Cross uses fabric softener.

LEO

Yeah but he's old.

EVERLY

He's not old, you douche.

HENDRIX

Whatever. It's not like it's hard to mix it up with bleach.

NIXON

Oh man, Henny . . .

EVERLY

Hey. You don't get to call him Henny. That's for me and Gracie.

NIXON

Thanks to your husband, we can't call you evil twin anymore.

LEO

Yeah. You're gonna have to share Henny, Evie.

GRACIE

Ummm . . . Hello . . . We've got dibs on Henny.

HENDRIX

Why are you on this text chain?

EVERLY

Damnit. Dinner was supposed to be a surprise.

NIXON

Might not want to text the group chat with her in it next time.

EVERLY

Fuck off. You have no clue what baby brain does to a person.

LEO

What?

HENDRIX

Holy Shit!

GRACIE

OMG!

NIXON

Dad's gonna lose his shit.

My twin sister is having a baby . . .
Wow.

Kerrigan and Jaxon are Cross's kids from a previous relationship, but as far as anyone is concerned, Everly is their mother. She adopted them once they were married. I never got to hold either of them when they were born.

I'm missing it all.

Ares

"God of war," Everly calls out from where's she's sitting on the porch swing on their back porch.

I pop my head through the open glass doors and laugh when I see the same book in her hands that Gracie had on the plane this morning. Jesus. Was that only this morning? Jet lag is a bitch when you're going backward.

London is five hours ahead of us. So even though it's eight o'clock our time, my body thinks it's midnight, and it's been up and going since stupid early o'clock.

"Did Cross tell you we're doing dinner soon?"

"Yeah. Is your whole family coming?" There's a fuck-ton of them.

"No. Just my brothers and Gracie and you and Bellamy . . . I think Caitlin was going to hang with Maddox, Callen, Brynn, and her brother tonight." She sips a sweet tea and frowns.

"What's wrong?"

"Nothing. Just stupid decaf. So . . ." she perks up. "You gonna tell us where you went on your mini-vacay?"

"Nope." Grace catches my eye as she walks up the beach path to the house. "But I'll be down for dinner. You need anything?"

"Nope." Everly yawns and stretches her arms above her head. "Cross just ran out to grab dinner. I think he's picking up some more alcohol. And you guys exhausted the kids on the beach today. They're already passed out. We should have a half hour before my brothers show up."

And like a mad scientist who's just been given the keys to the kingdom, I'm giddy at the idea of thirty minutes with a basically quiet, somewhat empty-ish house.

I can get a whole lot done when I set my mind to something.

And what I'm set to do just walked my way.

An old, worn, pink Hart & Soul t-shirt hides her white-and-pink-striped bikini and barely covers her perfect ass.

She climbs the stairs and excitedly hugs her sister as the two of them talk in hushed tones. *What the hell's that about?*

Gracie must say something Everly likes because she smacks Grace's ass and laughs. "Go shower before dinner. And be quiet upstairs. The kids are asleep."

I slip out before I can hear the rest of their conversation, having narrowed down exactly what I plan to do. And *with who*. And where.

This is gonna be fun.

---

*F*ive minutes later, the door to Grace's bedroom opens, and I cover her mouth when she steps in. At first, she looks like she's going to scream, but once my girl sees it's me, she shocks the shit out of me and jumps.

Legit jumps.

She throws her arms around my neck and her legs around my waist and crushes her mouth to mine. "We don't have long," she whispers. "You'd better start peeling."

Fuck, I love this woman.

I slide my hand into her hair and lock the door behind us, then walk us into the en suite bathroom and lock that door for extra measure. "Do you know what it was like watching you prance around in this all day?"

I sit her down on the vanity and run my hands up her ribs, pulling her pink tee over her head and groaning. Grace attacks my mouth, just as eager as I am. "Do you have any idea how close I came to killing every single fucker that looked at you today?"

Grace tugs my shirt over my head and throws it to the floor. "Says the man who spent twenty-five minutes talking to the hot lifeguard . . . Come on, was she even eighteen?" she teases, and I like this jealous side to her.

"You feeling possessive, good twin?" I lean back, turn the shower on, and wait for the water to get warm. "Because I sure as shit was all day. And I didn't like not being able to stake my claim."

She hops down off the counter, and her boobs bounce in her bikini top, and I almost come in my shorts like a thirteen-year-old kid. I reach for her, and she spins away. "You're goddamn right I'm feeling possessive, god of war. I waited nearly eight long months to call you mine. And you are mine."

She grabs my face and presses her lips to mine.

My blood roars, and she steps back and spins around, then gathers her hair in her hands and holds it on top of her head. "Want to help me with these ties, Ares?"

I take the ties around her neck in my fingers and pull, watching them fall. My lips graze her shoulder, and I bite down against her heated skin. "All fucking day, Grace . . . I've wanted to taste the salt on your skin all fucking day."

A small moan slips past her lips, and I untie the string in the center of her back and watch the tiny triangles drop to the floor. I pull her back against me and wrap my hands around her, cupping her breasts and dragging my thumbs over her nipples.

Grace hisses and shimmies her bikini bottoms down, then steps into the shower and turns to face me. "As much as I'm enjoying this, we've got to be quick before someone comes looking for us."

"Baby . . . You can't stand naked in front of me and expect me to give a shit about anyone else." My mouth goes dry as I stand there, staring at all her tanned skin. "I'm going to devour you."

I strip out of my shorts and add them to our pile, then move in behind her and adjust the showerheads to keep her wet and warm.

She backs up against me, and I force myself not to fuck her yet.

Not an easy thing.

I reach around her and grab her shampoo, then squeeze a few drops onto her head and massage it through her long hair. The citrusy scent swirls around us, and her entire body relaxes against mine.

"God, that feels good," she moans, and my cock weeps.

"It's only going to get better," I promise, then rinse the suds from her hair and watch with greedy eyes as they glide over her body. I drag my hands over her ribs and toned abs, then run my fingers through her smooth sex before she starts breathing heavy and spins around.

"My room. My shower. My turn," she scolds me and drops to her knees with a wicked smile on her face that I could get used to. I like this version of Grace. Her confidence is sexy.

She looks up at me through long lashes and heavily hooded eyes.

I run my fingers through her hair and push it away from her face, then rub my thumb over her jaw. "Possessive looks fucking amazing on you, baby. Now show me who you belong to."

The water pounds down over both of us while she fists the base of my throbbing cock and parts her lips, waiting for me to feed it to her. Then without hesitation, she swirls her tongue around the head and tries to tighten her grip.

A smug smile tugs at my lips when her hand can't quite wrap entirely around me.

I'm far from small. But she already knows she can handle me.

I wrap her hair around one fist and tug. I want her eyes on me.

She reaches up and wraps her hands around my ass, pulling me forward.

Taking me deeper.

And batting those fucking lashes until I nearly come on the spot.

"So fucking mine," I growl as thundering need licks down the base of my spine.

She flattens her tongue and drags it up the length of my cock, then pops off and licks her lips. "Then show me," she whispers with devious eyes, echoing my earlier words, and takes me all the way down her throat, moaning as I give her what she wants.

My abs pull tight, not ready to come yet, and I slam my hand against the cool tile wall, needing to come but wanting her tight cunt wrapped around me when I do.

"What's the matter?" she asks when I pull her head back like she thinks she did something wrong.

I lift her from her knees and wrap her legs around my hips. My cock kisses her entrance, pulling moans from both of us, and I press her back against the tile. "I fucking love you, Grace."

I bury my cock deep inside her, and Grace presses her forehead to mine. "Don't be gentle."

Her words rip something apart inside me, and I thrust up as I drag her down over me. Her tight, wet pussy clenches around me as I swallow each moan until she's clawing at my back, shaking as her orgasm rips through her body, and I follow her into oblivion.

The Philly Press

KROYDON KRONICLES

SINFUL SUMMER

The PuckPack is on the move, and O'Malley's seems to be the place to be. We might be missing the Wilder brothers, but I spy with my little eye enough Sinclairs to make up for our loss.

#PuckPack #SummerFun #KroydonKronicles

ARES

It's a weird thing to watch another family's dynamic, especially when you feel an overwhelming need to protect one of them. But I'm not the only one who thinks they need to protect Grace. It was obvious long before tonight that her brothers and sister all think it's their job to keep her safe. The difference tonight is that need to protect is instead pissing me off. If any one of them would open their eyes, they'd see Grace needs to protect herself.

They're not bad people. I'm actually enjoying watching them tease each other. It's like someone took Cross, Bellamy, and me and dialed us up to ten. They're nuts. It's like a trainwreck you just can't look away from.

But they've definitely placed Grace firmly in the *good twin* box.

None of them have any clue that twenty-four hours ago, my girl cried herself to sleep as I held her. They don't know she told me she hated her life. Or that she wasn't even sure she ever wanted to dance again.

They don't know any of it because she hasn't told them.

She played the part well. And I'm finally realizing it's a

part she's played her whole life, not one that's she's only stepping into now. This isn't new for her. And that knowledge is fucking frightening. Because I'm pretty sure her family being disappointed in her would be worse for Grace than any broken bone could ever be.

Bellamy's phone buzzes, and she checks a text as Cross glares like Dad would if we were back in Maine. "I can feel you yelling at me, Cross." She rolls her eyes, then does a happy dance. "Anyone want to go to O'Malley's? Caitlin just texted. She's going there now with Callen, Brynlee, and Maddox."

"Hell yeah, I'm going. I want to see Madman lose his mind when the first dude hits on Caitlin." Leo's grin is vicious, and I'm not gonna lie—I'm here for it. Because it's about time Maddox gets to be on the receiving end of shit from his sister.

"You coming, Ares?" Bellamy asks as she pushes up from her chair.

"Not tonight, B. I'm exhausted." Not exactly a lie. I'm tired as fuck. I'm also hoping Grace stays home.

"How about you, Gracie? Want to come out with us?" Hendrix grabs the back of Gracie's chair and leans over. "Come on. I've never gotten to drink with you."

"Umm . . . That's because you're not even twenty-one yet, Henny. You shouldn't even be going."

"Is it past the baby's bedtime?" Leo taunts, and Hendrix cheap-shots him.

"Aww . . . Do you want me to put you to bed with the other babies, Henny?" Everly teases as she stands from her chair and picks up his plate.

"Sit down, Everly," Cross orders, and the room goes deathly quiet as all eyes go to him.

My brother never gets loud.

"We have four brothers and two sisters in this room.

You've run after two kids all day, and you're pregnant. Let them get the goddamn dishes. I'm taking you to bed."

Cross tugs her hand, and Everly's smile is instantaneous. "I love it when you get bossy."

A chorus of *ewws* and *oh my Gods* echoes around the room as everyone fights to get the plates and get the hell out of dodge as quickly as possible before any of us have to see more of the Cross and Everly peep show than we've already seen over the past year.

Seriously. More than enough.

It doesn't take long for everyone to pile into the kitchen with the dishes. "Go. I've got this," Grace tells them. "Don't do anything stupid."

"Callen is gonna be there. He brings the stupid with him," Nixon tries to calm her worry, but I don't think it works.

"Never good when you're comparing yourself to Callen, Nix," she snickers.

He drops a kiss on her head, then smacks Leo and Hendrix on the back of their heads. "Whose driving? Bellamy and I don't have a car."

Leo tosses Hendrix his keys. "Sucks to be the youngest, Henny."

"Don't fucking call me Henny, you douche."

Bellamy grabs her purse and keys. "I'm not sure where Cait and I are gonna crash tonight. So don't wait up."

"Don't get pregnant," I tell her and shut the front door behind her before she can give me a smart-ass answer.

By the time I walk back into the kitchen, Grace is turning the dishwasher on. Her dark hair is in loose waves down around her bare shoulders. And the moonlight filtering in casts a silvery glow over her flowy white sundress that hits just above her knees.

I walk up behind her and wrap my arms around her waist

and brush my lips over hers when she turns her face to me. "You doing okay?"

She nods. "Why wouldn't I be?"

"Your family was asking a lot of questions tonight." I slide my hands down her thighs, then drag them back up, bringing her dress with them.

Grace shivers and sighs a long, lazy sound. "It's fine. I have to figure out what I'm doing before I can tell them anything anyway."

I trace the seam of her panties, feeling her heat soaking through, and her breathing becomes anything but lazy. "My sister could come downstairs and catch us," she warns me before she leans back, wraps a hand around my neck, and leans against my chest as I slide her panties aside.

"She's busy," I whisper and drag my finger through her sex, then trace the dampness all over her pussy. "Kinda like you're gonna be, baby."

"Oh, God," slips out almost silently as I press my finger inside her, and fuck, I like that sound. "I think I'm going to like sneaking around if it's always this hot."

"Uncle Ares?"

Oh fuck.

Grace and I break apart immediately, and I look over at my four-year-old niece. "Hey, Kerrigan. What are you doing up?"

"I was thirsty," she tells me innocently. Only her *th* sounds more like an *f* sound.

I move behind the island, so my sweet niece isn't traumatized by my raging boner while Grace grabs her a juice box. "Here you go, little miss. Do you want me to tuck you in?"

Kerrigan nods her head dramatically and takes Grace's hand to lead her out of the room.

Yup. I was just cockblocked by a toddler.

Thirty minutes later, when Grace hasn't come back

downstairs, I decide to go on a scouting mission. It doesn't take long to find her. But unfortunately for me, she's not in her bed. Hell, she's not even in mine. Nope. My girl is tucked in next to Kerrigan in a giant princess bed.

Fitting for both of them.

Guess I'm sleeping alone tonight.

GRACE

༄

I'm not sure how long I've been in Kerrigan's bed when a stuffed bunny to the face wakes me. But the mini-Wilder, who's already stolen a piece of my heart, is sleeping like a little angel—a violent little angel who flips over and kicks my hip as she starfishes across the bed. But she's still a very cute, violent, little angel.

I take that as my cue and carefully slide out of one bed I don't belong in and tiptoe down the hall to another.

Ares's closed door is the one before mine, and my hand hovers over the knob I'm about to open when Bellamy and Caitlin come to a stop at the top of the stairs, clearly drunk. They stumble and laugh, and I quickly yank my hand back and glare at the two of them. "Be quiet. The babies are sleeping." Then I stare at them when they try not to laugh. "You didn't drive, did you?"

They both stop in their tracks, and while Caitlin looks caught, Bellamy looks intrigued.

"No, we didn't drive. Nixon made Hendrix drive everyone home." She tries to point at me but ends up smacking herself with her purse in the process, then recovers and frowns. "Bossy Nix is kinda hot."

"Eww." I try to ignore that thought. "Whatever you say."

I wait them out to see if they're going to wake the kids up. Well, that's my excuse. Really, I need them to go to bed so I can slip into Ares's room without getting caught. But apparently, Bellamy isn't as drunk as I originally thought.

"You're the next room down, Grace. Which one of us had too much to drink?" She laughs it off, but there's something in her tone.

"Oops. I just woke up and snuck out of Kerrigan's room. Thanks." I step back.

Then a devious grin spreads across Caitlin's face. "I wouldn't mind accidentally sleeping in Ares's bed."

"Hands off my brother." Bellamy scrunches up her face and pushes Caitlin into their shared bedroom, then stops and watches me like she doesn't trust me to go to my room. *What's up with that?* "Goodnight, Grace."

Guess that means I'll be sleeping alone tonight.

The next morning, Everly and I are sitting at the table on the back deck, sipping decaf—which, by the way, tastes like shit on principal alone—when Brynlee walks out with Callen and Maddox. She drops a box of cinnamon rolls on the table and pushes them my way, and Everly and I both stop and stare at her in sync.

"What did you do that you're bribing me with sweets, Brynnie?" I ask very slowly, afraid of just how bad her answer will be.

"So . . ." Brynn pulls out a chair and takes her time sitting down.

Apparently, she's not fast enough for Maddox though. "Listen,"—he grabs a cinnamon roll and takes a bite—"Callen and I are going to swap apartments with Brynn. She doesn't need all that space anymore, but we could use it. So you'll be moving into our condo." He takes another bite and smirks at Brynn. "See? Wasn't that hard."

"I'm getting coffee," Callen groans, and Everly laughs.

"It's decaf . . ." Everly calls after him.

"Fuck," he mutters as he disappears into the kitchen.

Meanwhile, I stare, dumbfounded, at Brynlee. My mouth opens and closes like the pretty, *non-food* fish Kerrigan wants. "Did you just *Friends* us?" I ask, unsure if I'm asking Brynn or Maddox. "Because there's no way you'd give up that condo for theirs. Is there?"

"Don't ask," she murmurs and stuffs an entire pastry in her mouth, then shoves them my way. "Try them," she says around a mouth full of food. "They're good."

Everly laughs so hard I kick her chair, but she doesn't care. "Dude. You're going to be sleeping where so many women have slept before. I hope you clean that place with bleach before you touch any surfaces. Seriously, girls. Beware of STDs. I bet some of them are even airborne."

"I fucking hate you," Brynlee tells Maddox, who's grinning like the bastard he likes to pretend he is.

"Honest to God. One of you had better tell me what I missed," I try to demand, but it falls on deaf ears when they both ignore me, and Everly picks up my phone and types in my password. Because, of course, she knows what it is.

"What the hell are you doing?" I ask.

"Door Dashing bleach to your new condo. You're gonna need a lot of it."

I'd love to say us swapping condos with the guys was a joke or some kind of 90s sitcom thing gone horrifically wrong. But it wasn't. It was all-hands-on-deck as we spent all day Sunday packing up the penthouse Lindy, Kenzie, Everly, Brynlee, and I had shared for years while the guys move everything down to their place, then brought their stuff up to what used to be ours.

I may not have lived here for the better part of the past year, but it still hurts my heart. We loved decorating this place. Picking each new piece and color. It doesn't feel like it was that long ago, but in reality, two of us are moms now, Brynlee has been Dr. St. James since we moved in, and Kenzie is officially Dr. Hayes now.

Life moved on, and we all grew up.

And I'm not sure I like that realization.

Luckily, it didn't take as long as I expected it to. No one can get an answer out of Callen, Maddox, or Brynlee about why the hell she agreed to the swap—and we've all tried. Even Bellamy and Caitlin got in on it with no luck. They said one minute they were doing shots at the bar, and the next thing they knew, Maddox and Brynlee were arguing.

Once the last of the boxes has been moved out, I stand in the middle of my old bedroom and try not to be sad. I was never supposed to be coming back here anyway.

"Hey, beautiful." Ares quietly sneaks in and closes the door behind himself. "You doing okay?"

I nod, a little too choked up to answer.

"Hey, now. What's wrong?" He tugs me against his chest and fits my head under his chin. "Why do you look so sad?"

"I'm not sure. Everything is just changing so fast."

"Maybe it'll be easier to sneak in and out of your place now that you're next to mine." He lifts my chin and presses a quick kiss to my lips, and I immediately want more.

I wrap my arms around his waist and pull him closer. "I like the sound of that."

"Gracie—" Nixon shouts as he bangs on my bedroom door, and I jump five feet.

"*Shit*. Go hide," I tell Ares and push him toward my closet.

"You're fucking kidding, right?"

When I push him back another step, he loses his smile. "You're not kidding?"

"No," I hush him and shove him into my closet. "I'm not. Now be quiet." I close him in and call out, "It's open, Nix."

The knob twists, but the door doesn't open. "It's not. It's locked."

"Oops. One sec." I swing the door open. "I'm almost done." I look around my empty room and point to the remaining box. "Think you could take that downstairs for me?"

"Sure. You know, it might be nice having you next door for a few months, good twin."

Oh, Nixon. If only you knew I was hiding your roommate in my closet.

"It'll be fun." I smile and wait for him to leave.

"Ares and I are thinking about going to West End to grab dinner after this. You wanna come?"

"With you . . . and Ares?" My stomach flips. I never used to think I was a liar. But I sure as hell am now. "No, thanks. Brynn and I are going to try to get settled. Maybe another night."

"Do you know who else is moving in with Madman and Callen, now that they got all this space?" Nixon asks, not at all taking the hint that I need him to leave.

"No. I didn't ask." Mainly because I'm too pissed they're

getting our place at all. The perfect lighting. The two floors. The easy access to the rooftop. *Assholes.*

"Yeah. Me either. They didn't say when I asked them earlier. It was kinda weird."

I shrug, trying to move him along, but he waits for me. Why are men so damn dense? "Listen, I just need a minute, then I'll be down, okay?"

"Sure, good twin." Nixon picks up the box and looks around the room. "It's bigger than my room at Ares's place."

"Get out now, Nixon. I swear to God, if you move into my old bedroom, I'll tell you in great detail every single guy I screwed in here."

"What the fuck is wrong with you?" He makes a disgusted sound and storms out. "Fucking gross."

I close the door and lock it for good measure. "He's gone."

Ares bursts out of my closet and grabs my face. "If I ever hear you talk about fucking another man again, I'll have you over my goddamned knee so fast, you'll see stars before I ever let you orgasm."

Sweet baby Jesus in a manger. Yes, please.

"Do you understand me, baby?"

"Fuck yes, I do, and I want that. *All* of that." I slide up to my toes and suck his lip between mine before pushing my tongue in. "I want it now," I pant because that's what he does to me. Damn.

Ares takes control of our kiss. His hand wraps around my throat and slides it up to my jaw, and holy hotness, I want to bend over right here, right now.

"Better figure out a way to sneak me into your room tonight, good twin." He smacks my ass so hard, I know there's a red hand print on my cheek, and I squeak.

"Yes, sir."

"I like it. Let's play with that later." He walks over to the door and listens for a second before he opens it and slips out.

"Tonight, Grace." And then he's gone, and I'm left standing here wet and wanting. Damn, my man is hot.

Once it's just Brynn and me in the guys' old condo, which I still refuse to call *our* new condo, I try one last time to get the goods. "Come on, Brynnie. Spill it. You loved that place. What happened to make you swap?"

"Listen," she tells me as she yanks green and pink rubber gloves up to her elbows and dumps out the cleaning supplies on the kitchen counter. "It doesn't matter. What matters now is that this is the new condo, and I'm so excited you're here with me for the summer, Grace. Now grab a pair of gloves and get cleaning. This place smells like Callen's dirty gym socks."

Brynlee St. James is just as much a Kingston heiress as Lindy.

But unlike Lindy, you'd never know it if Brynn didn't tell you herself.

Her mother, Scarlet, is the oldest Kingston sister, and she's the general manager for the Philadelphia Kings, as well as part owner of the Revolution.

Then there's her dad . . . Cade St. James. The dad we all had stars in our eyes over every time we went to her house as young girls. He's a former MMA heavyweight champion, and he's gorgeous. Like *gor-geous*. And together, Cade and Scarlet have always done their best to give each of their kids as normal a life as possible, which definitely shows in how Brynn lives her life.

Right about now, I wish she'd at least be open to hiring

someone to come and clean though. But to Brynn, cleaning is cathartic, and she's about to make this place her bitch.

"Whatever you say, crazy lady." I yank the gloves up and wait for my orders as she sprays something all over the kitchen countertops.

"Listen, it just made sense. That's all. You're only staying a few weeks, and I don't need a five-bedroom condo all to myself. You've all moved out and moved on, and I'm the only one left here. So help me make this place livable."

She passes me a bucket filled with supplies for the bathroom, and I take it with a groan. "Seriously? Can't we hire someone to do this?"

Brynn stops and looks at me. "Sure we can. And while we're waiting for them to get here, you can tell me what the hell is going on with you and the god of war because we haven't had five minutes alone to talk since you got back. And you better believe I didn't miss the fact that you two showed up together."

"Fine. I'll scrub the damn bathroom." Anything to not have this conversation.

"Bathrooms, Grace." She waits with her brows raised. "There's two of them."

"I hate you," I grumble and walk away.

"We're still going to talk about it, good twin."

GRACE

                                GRACE

> You are disgusting.

EVERLY

You're going to need to be more specific, Gracie.

KENZIE

Ohh . . . Who's disgusting?

                                  GRACE

> Oops. I sent this to the wrong chat. Hold please.
>
> Okay, Callen and Maddox have now been added to the chat.

LINDY

Dude. Make sure you remove their asses after this. I don't want to talk about sucking my husband's dick with the guys on the text.

MADDOX

WTF? I don't want to know that shit.

CALLEN

Sweet. Let's hear it.

EVERLY

What is wrong with you?

CALLEN

I'm not related to her and she's HOT AF. Come on, Lindy. Let's hear it.

LINDY

Is this why they're disgusting?

MADDOX

Whose disgusting?

GRACE

You! When was the last time you assholes cleaned?

BRYNLEE

Better question - Why don't you have a cleaning lady?

KENZIE

Wait . . . I know the answer. Callen fucked her, then called her the wrong name.

EVERLY

OMG. Seriously? Your balls are going to shrivel up from some dirty disease, Callen.

CALLEN

I wrap it up every single time. Thank you very much.

GRACE

And that's why you're gross. I found your condoms.

CALLEN

Safe sex, good twin. You should try it.

GRACE

THEY WERE USED!

EVERLY

OMG.

LINDY

Shame on your house!

KENZIE

. . . I just threw up in my mouth.

CALLEN

But did you swallow?

KENZIE

I fucking hate you.

MADDOX

You're a doctor. You've seen worse.

BRYNLEE

I hate you too.

CALLEN

Did you happen to find any unused condoms, Grace? I was looking for my box while we were unpacking.

Callen has been removed from the conversation.

LINDY

Get rid of Maddox too.

Maddox has been removed from the conversation.

> EVERLY
>
> Good. Never let them in our sacred space again.
>
> BRYNLEE
>
> Okay, Mother Earth.

I close out of my phone and get out of the tub I've been soaking in for the past thirty minutes. I'm not sure I've ever felt grimier than I did when we finished scrubbing this place. But now it smells fresh and looks clean, and Brynn and I are going to do a little shopping tomorrow to warm it up a bit.

The boys had boring taste.

But at least they had expensive boring taste.

The heated floors are a nice touch.

I slip into my fuzzy white robe and tie it at the waist, then flop down on my bed with no intention of moving for the rest of the night.

"Hey." Brynn pops her head in my room. "I'm heading out."

"You look pretty. Going somewhere fun?"

She walks over and tugs my hair out of the messy bun I threw it in so it wouldn't get wet, then tousles it.

"What the hell?"

"Don't ask me where I'm going, and I won't ask you why Ares is standing in our new living room."

"What?" I sit right up with that new nugget of information.

What part of under the radar does he not get?

"Wait . . . so you're going to see a man?" I mean, if she's saying she won't ask about Ares if I don't—

Brynn shakes her head and places her pointer finger in front of her lips. "See you bright and early tomorrow for your evaluation, good twin." She winks and walks away, leaving me intrigued until I remember I'm annoyed.

"Under the radar, god of war," I mumble as I fix my robe. And okay, maybe I flip my hair upside down for a little extra body like Brynn tried to do before I march into the living room.

"You left this in my truck the other day. I thought you might need it for tomorrow." Ares is standing and looking smug with my ballet bag in his hand.

I'm not sure what steals my bravado more . . . the fact that he has a legitimate reason to be here or that he's standing in front of me, freshly showered with damp hair, smelling like sandalwood and cedar, wearing sweats and one of those tanks with the long arm openings. The kind that showcase every golden muscle and the colorful ink on his incredible arms and delicious lats.

"Is that the only reason you're here?" Pretty sure I just drooled. Definitely licked my lips.

"What else did you have in mind, beautiful?" He drops my bag to the floor and takes a step forward.

"Oh, I have a few ideas . . . sir."

In the next moment, the air whooshes from my lungs when Ares hoists me over his shoulder like a fireman and smacks my ass so hard I may have just dripped on him. *Holy shit.*

His hand caresses my stinging cheek as he walks toward my bedroom. "Have you been a bad girl, Gracie?"

"Yes, sir . . ."

Ares

I kick the door shut behind us before lying her down on the bed. Her soft little robe slides open, and her creamy breasts tease me in a way only Grace ever has.

She's temptation personified.

And I'm going to indulge all fucking night.

I drop a knee on the bed and shove her robe off her shoulders, enjoying the way her breathing picks up. "I could spend an eternity worshipping you, and it wouldn't be enough time."

"Show me," she challenges, and I willingly accept.

I crawl down her delicious body and wedge my shoulders between her splayed legs.

"You want to be punished, baby?" I untie her sash and lick my way down her golden skin, fucking desperate for her. The way she responded to me earlier . . . *Fuck me.* I've been hard since. I tried jacking off in the shower, but my body protested. I don't want to come in my hand. I want to come in her cunt. Her mouth. I want to bathe her in it until no one ever questions whose woman she is.

"Yes, sir," she pants, and I slide my hand between her thighs and slap her pussy.

"Ohmygod," she cries out and closes her legs around my hand.

I crawl down her body and between her pretty legs, peppering kisses along her bare pussy. "You sure?" I tease and spread her wide with my thumbs, licking a line up her hot center.

She moans, and I stop.

"Answer me, Grace."

"Whatever it was, yes. Yes, I want it. *You.* Please. The answer is yes."

I'd laugh if I didn't love that she's already writhing

beneath me, and I've barely touched her. I bury my face in her cunt, coating my face with her juices and sucking her clit between my lips until she's crying out.

Then I stop.

"What?" she cries out, and I smile.

"Fuck, baby. Your skin is all pink and flushed. So fucking pretty." Yeah. I'm gonna edge the hell out of my tiny dancer for what she said to her brother earlier. And I'm gonna fucking love every minute of it.

Grace whimpers a sexy little sound that goes straight to my already rock-hard cock. I throw one smooth leg over my shoulder, opening her to me, and fucking feast on her with my teeth and tongue and fingers until her back bows off the bed. I swear her screams could wake the whole building.

"Fuck, *yes*. Right there." She buries her hands in my hair and holds me where she wants me, as she grinds against my face with desperate pleas. "Don't you dare stop."

She's so fucking sexy like this.

Taking what she wants.

Not worrying about pleasing anyone but herself.

Tonight, I'm going to give her what she wants. But she's gonna have to work for it first.

When her breathing picks up and her walls clench around me, I throw her other leg over my shoulder and grab her ass in both hands, pulling her closer as I plunge my tongue into her core, over and over until she shakes. Then I stop and stand up with a big fucking smile on my face.

"What the hell—"

"Not yet, Grace," I warn, and a fire lights behind her eyes.

"Not yet?" she asks with shaky breath.

"No, beautiful. Not yet."

Grace's eyes slide down my body to where my cock tents my sweats. "You look overdressed, god of war."

"You want to help me with that?" I ask, forcing myself to

stay balanced on the tightrope I'm walking right now. Because fuck, all I want to do is bury myself inside her. But I want to spend the entire night worshipping this woman more.

Grace crawls across the bed on her hands and knees, then sits up and flattens her palms under my shirt and up my abs. "This?" she asks. "You want me to take this off?"

I gently drag only the tips of my fingers down her spine, enjoying the way she shakes, then smack her ass again and watch her knees nearly buckle. "Yeah, baby. Take it off me."

She shoves my shirt over my head, then presses her bare breasts against my naked chest and crushes her mouth to mine. Her hands dive back into my hair, and my girl takes complete control of the kiss. She drags her mouth down my neck and over my abs until she's crawled off the bed and is standing in front of me. She grips my waistband as she drops to her knees, bringing my sweats down with her.

"Going commando tonight, Ares? Awfully confident."

I gather her long hair in my hand and wrap it around my knuckles.

Can't have anything fucking with the view of my woman on her knees for me.

"If I had to wait to sneak into your room at three a.m., I would have. Two nights without you was two nights too many, baby."

Grace preens at my words, and her smile wraps around me like a tether.

I'm never letting this girl go.

She grips my dick in her fist, then wraps those pink lips around me and moans.

Fucking moans.

Like she's been dying without me the way I've been without her.

"God, you're fucking beautiful like this." Her sexy, sweet

hum of approval vibrates straight down my spine. "With that pretty fucking mouth on me."

Grace Sinclair has quickly become so much more than I ever knew she could be.

And she's mine.

She looks up at me through her dark lashes, her aqua eyes glistening with unshed tears pooling in them, and swallows me deeper. She cups my balls with her other hand, and my entire body coils tight.

"Are you a good girl, Gracie?"

She nods her head and moans around me.

"Touch yourself, beautiful."

Her eyes fly up to mine, scared.

"Have you ever touched yourself in front of someone before, Grace?"

She shakes her head and swallows me down her throat.

"I want you to slide your fingers in your pussy."

"Ares," she whines, not sure if she wants to do it.

"Don't stop sucking, Gracie."

My girl takes me back into her hot mouth and slides her hand between her legs.

"Dip them inside yourself. Get them nice and wet, then I want you to rub them around your clit, Grace. Don't touch it though." My body tightens at the erotic site in front of me.

Fuck.

She's a vision.

I tug her hair tighter. "Do. Not. Come, Grace."

She hums her approval, and I nearly come on the spot before she takes one of my hands and puts it on the back of her head. Then she takes me so fucking deep, I see an entire galaxy of stars.

I let go of her hair and drag my other hand over her head, gently thrusting my hips. "You okay, beautiful?"

Grace practically purrs around me as she works herself faster while I fuck her face.

"Don't come, Grace," I warn, and the fucking sound that rips from her throat is beautiful frustration. "Trust me, baby."

She pulls her hand from her body and drags her nails up the backs of my thighs and over my ass. I close my eyes and remind myself I'm edging us both right now.

She pops off my dick and licks a long lazy path from my balls to the head, then takes me back down her throat, and I pull myself out of her mouth.

Fuck.

Something inside me snaps.

I lift her from her knees and toss her onto the bed with a bounce. "Are you ever going to talk about another man in front of me again, Gracie?"

She leans up on her elbows, and her heavy, lust-fueled eyes lock on mine. "There will never be another man. I only want you, god of war."

"Fucking phenomenal answer." I run a hand down her body and grip her hips as my mouth captures hers.

"Now you're ready for me, baby." I flip her over to her knees and smack her ass, leaving a bright-red handprint that I run my tongue over.

"Ares," she moans my name, and goddamn, I like that sound.

"Damn. You look even prettier with my handprint on your skin, baby."

Grace mewls and pushes her ass back into my hand. "More, Ares . . . Please."

I drag a thumb through the wetness dripping down the inside of her creamy thighs, then push it back inside her, and she drops her forehead to the bed on a desperate plea.

"Ass in the air, baby." My hand slides over her hip while I drag the thick head of my cock through her drenched sex.

She turns her head to watch me, and I push into her in a hard thrust, then pull out and do it again. Watching my cock disappear into her pretty pussy as a guttural moan rips from somewhere deep in my body.

Her lids flutter shut as she drops her head back to the bed.

"Eyes on me, beautiful. Watch me fuck you. Tell me how it feels." I wrap and arm around her and pull her up to her knees, so her back is against my chest. Not a millimeter of room between us.

Grace slings an arm back and drapes it around my neck as I drag my mouth over hers.

My hands slide down her body and over her nipples. Tweaking them. Pinching them. Drawing every sexy sound I can out of my girl. Feeding my addiction. I drag them down to her waist and grip tightly as I control her body with each snap of my hips.

Grace arches her back, and I trail my tongue over her spine.

"I'm so close, Ares. I need to come." Her voice shakes with such an intense fucking need, I want nothing more than to give us what we both crave, but I'm far from done with her yet.

I snap my hips against hers, holding her against me, worshipping her like I desperately need to. Fucking her slow and hard until her body sings and my muscles burn. Then I drag my lips over the shell of her ear. "Not yet, baby. Bad girls don't get to come *yet*."

GRACE

"Ares," I cry in devastation when he pulls out.

Until his mouth is on mine an instant later. Hot and hard. His tongue tangling with mine.

"Are you gonna be a good girl next time?" he whispers, and I purr with contentment as his words and his breath wash over my skin.

"Yes," I whimper, trembling and so needy for him. For the release only he can give me.

"Lie down, Grace."

He'll never know what his voice alone is capable of.

The way it turns me on. The things it does to my body.

With what little control I have left, I turn and lie down against the cool sheets and arch my back, pushing my breasts up into Ares's hands and loving the way he swallows and growls as he runs his rough thumbs over my nipples.

I'd love to say two can play at this game, but I'm in so far over my head, I might as well be playing in a different league altogether.

His fingers skim over my hot, sticky skin as he grins the

sexiest fucking smile I've ever seen. "If you don't make me come soon, I might actually die, god of war."

"Oh, you're gonna come, but only when I say you can, and you're gonna fucking love it."

He drags his cock through my swollen sex, coating himself in my wetness. Wetness that's been building for what feels like hours since I've lost all track of time and space.

He pushes in the tiniest bit, then pulls back again, and I reach up and claw at his chest as I try desperately to bring him down to me. "I want to feel your weight on me. I need you so bad," I pant as he pushes in again, then pulls back out.

Ares's eyes light up with an unmistakable need, which makes me feel so entirely feminine. Desired and beautiful. He reaches down and pulls one nipple into his mouth as he pinches the other one, and a wanton moan slips past my lips. Long and loud and absolutely frantic for more.

He laces his fingers with mine, and his body against me feels right.

Like I was made to be his.

He kisses me, and the world stands still around us.

I'm breathless and silent and entirely destroyed by the absolute tenderness he shows in one moment, followed by another slap to my pussy before he fills me in one long, hard, slow thrust.

I lift my hips and close my eyes and get lost in all the delicious sensations of being filled so completely by this man. The way he stretches me so fully. The way he touches me without worrying I'm going to break.

"Open your eyes, Grace. Watch me fuck you."

That voice. That tone. That command.

My eyes fly open, locking with his, then I wrap a hand around his neck, anchoring myself to him.

My true north.

"I need you, Ares."

"You have me, baby. You always will."

His body covers mine. His hands reverently caressing each dip and flare. Each curve and every long, lean muscle. His mouth presses against the hollow of my neck, sending crazy goosebumps over my hot skin.

He pulls us to our sides without losing our connection and drapes my leg over his hip, hitting an entirely new angle. *Fuck*. It's too much.

He takes his time. Dragging out each stroke of his cock.

Every pinch of his fingers on my clit sends electrical pulses through me.

I'm completely at his mercy.

"I can't . . ." I whimper incoherently.

"You can, beautiful. You will. I want you to tell me—how does it feel, baby?"

"Tight." He drags his cock along my oversensitive walls. "And hot."

His tongue pushes into my mouth. Claiming me. Owning me.

"I feel like I'm on the edge of the world, waiting to jump into oblivion," I pant, and he rolls his hips against mine.

"So full . . ."

Another snap of his hips, and my orgasm is right there, just out of reach.

"And oh my God, so fucking good."

He turns my face to his, owning my mouth, and I moan and mewl and cry.

It's too much but might not ever be enough.

"Don't stop," I plead over and over and over again as I cling to him.

"Fucking never, Grace." Then a switch flips in Ares, and he fucks me like a man possessed.

Harder.

Faster.

Driving me higher and higher.

"Give it to me, Grace. Give me everything." He snaps his hips against mine and wraps his hand around my throat. "I want your body. Your heart. I want your fucking soul," he growls.

I'm so hypersensitive, I'm basically an exposed nerve. One loud, thundering heartbeat pumping in time with his until I crest and shatter and come, absolutely destroyed.

"You were made for me, baby." He fucks me through my orgasm and turns my face, demanding my mouth. His tongue dominates me. "All fucking mine," he groans.

And just when I think I can't possibly take another second, Ares slams his hips up one last time, and I scream out as another orgasm violently rips through me.

He follows me over the cliff and comes inside me, his mouth continuing to worship mine.

"I'm yours, Ares. All yours. Only yours."

We lie there, tangled in each other.

Both of us trying desperately to catch our breaths.

He presses his lips to my temple. My chin. My lips.

"So fucking pretty, baby," he whispers against my skin.

"So fucking yours, god of war," I echo back.

I feel my eyes closing when he gets up quietly and walks into my bathroom. Minutes later, a warm, wet washcloth is pressed against my aching pussy, and my eyes fly open to find his. "Sleep, Grace."

"Will you stay with me?" I whisper and grab his hand.

He pulls back the blanket, climbs in next to me, and covers us both. Then, just as I'm drifting back off to sleep, he whispers, "Gonna have to tell Bryn about us."

"Hmm," I answer because that's pretty much all I'm capable of now. "She basically knows."

"Good. Because as long as I get to have you, I want you

right here next to me. Tell her or not, but this is where I'm gonna be."

I hum my agreement—too tired to think of all the reasons why we can't work and too happy to worry about any of it now anyway—and sink into the safety of Ares's arms.

"You've got to be kidding me." I sit up on Brynlee's exam table and stare in shock. "Come on, Brynn. We don't have to worst-case it here."

She stands across from me in her red Revolution polo with her pretty strawberry-blonde hair pulled up, showcasing the scowl on her face. "I'm looking at your scans here, Gracie, and it *is* borderline worst-case scenario. How did you dance with this for so long? You had to have been in serious pain."

I swing my legs over the table to jump off, and she stops me. "Listen to me. You can't just jump off this table. You've got to keep your weight off your foot."

I must not look thrilled because she turns the tablet toward me and points at the scan, pissed off. "Gracie. This is bad. This can do permanent damage. It may already have."

"What do you mean by keep my weight off my foot?" Just the thought of it makes me squirmy.

"For the first week, I want you to keep all weight-bearing activities off that foot. You need to use a crutch when you walk. And absolutely no dancing. You need to modify your stretching routine so you can continue doing that for the next few weeks. And I want you to add some isometric work in with it." She places the iPad down on her desk and sits down in front of her laptop. Her fingers fly across the keyboard while she's looking at me. "I'm going to write up a plan for you—because all of this *has* to be non-weight-bearing."

"For how long, Brynn?"

Her fingers stop moving, and she looks up at me. She's in Dr. St. James-mode right now. And I can tell right away, I'm not going to like what she has to say. "You're realistically looking at five to eight weeks minimum, Gracie."

"Five weeks," I gasp in complete denial. "I can't go five weeks without dancing."

She walks over to a closet and steps inside. "My educated guess is it's going to be closer to eight weeks. We'll do everything we can though." When she comes out, she's holding a box. "And you'll need to be in an air boot."

"Come on . . . You can't be serious. Brynn, I was dancing a week ago."

"You were hurting yourself a week ago. No wonder you're popping pain pills."

"What?" I gasp.

Brynn sits down next to me, shoulder to shoulder. "You popped more Aleve yesterday than most people take in two days. You're in pain, Grace. We need to manage the entire problem so it doesn't get worse. Masking the pain won't do that."

"It's over-the-counter, Brynn."

"It is. And you're going to need to continue to take it. But not that much. We're going to add in corticosteroid injections too. We'll manage it all, Grace. But you've got to do what I say. And you've got to stay off that foot. You said you told your company you'd be out for eight weeks. That means we've got seven weeks to try to get you where you need to be. And I think we can do it. But you've got to trust me."

I nod my head silently. Because words completely fail me.

She opens up the air boot and slips it onto my foot. "How does that feel?"

"Like a death sentence."

"It's not that bad. I had one for half a soccer season in high school, remember?" Brynn picks up my discarded sneaker and stuffs it in her bag. "Come on. Let's go drown your sorrows in Sweet Temptations cupcakes."

"I'd rather have West End cheeseburgers," I tell her as I carefully maneuver getting off this stupid table in this stupider boot. *Fuck.*

"Nope. Still too pissed off at Maddox for the condo thing. Compromise with The Busy Bee?"

"Fine," I agree, too upset to fight her. "Five weeks?"

"Minimum. I want you to plan for eight."

If I can't dance for eight weeks, my spot in London is gone.

I'll never be good enough to get my spot back after that.

Not there.

My heart sinks as Brynn leads me out of her exam room in the Revolution facility.

Eight weeks without dance *is* a death sentence for a dancer.

I'm sitting on the couch that night when someone knocks on our door, then lets themselves in. Only when I look over toward the door, it's not someone. It's several someones.

Maddox and Callen walk in, carrying takeout from West End, and they're followed by Nixon, Ares, Bellamy, and Caitlin. "What are you guys doing here?"

When everyone starts speaking at the same time, I hold my hand up and decide to ignore everyone who isn't Maddox or Callen. "You two—speak. And keep in mind that you now have my condo."

"Listen, good twin." Madman sits down next to me and stretches his arm out along the back of the couch. "You didn't live there anymore anyway. Brynn was in the big place by herself. And technically, King Corp. owns both condos. So really, they're communal family condos."

He palms the back of my head and starts massaging my scalp, and I don't want to enjoy it, but Maddox was always good at that. "Fine. But do the two of you really need that much space?"

"I think Killer is gonna move in with us. He's gotta get out of Cade and Scarlet's place before he loses his shit."

"Killer?" Bellamy questions.

"Yeah. Brynn's brother Killian. He's a year older than me," Caitlin tells her. "I thought Maverick said he wanted to move in if you ended up with the bigger place."

I turn, and daggers might as well be shooting from my eyes. "You knew?"

"Don't kill the messenger. I just heard a rumor," Cait snaps back.

"Maverick's living in the hockey house with Leo and Hendrix. I doubt he's leaving until he graduates," Nixon argues as he brings paper plates over to the coffee table and starts pulling the food out of the bags. He plates a cheeseburger deluxe with white cheddar cheese and a side of truffle fries and hands them to me. "Brynn texted and told us you might want to eat your feelings tonight."

Callen hands me an ice-cold sweet tea with a kiss-assy smile. "Evie can't make it. She's got a baby doctor appointment, and Lindy said the baby is puking his guts up. So it looks like you're stuck with us tonight."

I begrudgingly take my favorite drink from his hand and look around the room. My eyes briefly linger on Ares, whose stare is comforting and disconcerting all at once.

"Thanks, guys." I take a big bite of the greasy goodness and watch as everyone makes themselves at home, like they've always done in our condo. Guess it doesn't really matter which one it is.

"So this Killian . . . is he hot?" Bellamy asks, and I choke on a fry.

"He's gorgeous," I tell her and watch Ares's glare tighten. "He looks just like his dad."

My smile might be a little evil. But come on. It's been a shit day, and after last night, I wouldn't hate being punished again.

ARES

I thought my days of sneaking in and out of my bedroom ended when I left for the minors at eighteen. Back then, the thrill of not getting caught was half the damn fun back then. But after a few weeks of sneaking out of Grace's bed at the ass crack of dawn, so none of our roommates realize what we're doing, I'm over this shit.

I lean over Grace's naked body and brush a kiss over her cheek. "I'm going back to my place, baby."

She hums a happy sound and sinks her face into my pillow. And okay. Knowing she does that every time I leave eases the sting a little. But not enough. I walk as quietly as possible out into the girl's living room, then stop dead in my tracks.

"Oh shit." I close my eyes and turn away as fast as possible because Brynn is straddling some dude on the couch. Naked. I don't catch him. But sure as shit, it's Brynn. "Sorry. Just leaving."

"Get out," she yells, and I blindly walk toward the door with my hand stuck out in front of my face, so I don't kill myself in the process. Holy fucking shit. I've never been so goddamned glad to walk out of a door before.

I pull it shut behind me, then lean back and laugh.

Yeah . . . Gracie and I are gonna have to talk about this shit now. Because until about sixty seconds ago, she and Brynlee had a *don't ask, don't tell* kind of agreement happening. Brynn didn't want to be put in the middle of anything. So she played dumb, and in return, Grace didn't ask her about her mystery man. Grace's words. Not mine. It's worked for them for the last month and a half, but I'm pretty sure that just blew up in her face.

I just want to go the hell back to bed and catch a few hours of sleep before Nixon and I have to meet Cross and Easton for the practice session we've got planned for tomorrow. Training camp starts the third week in September, so we still have about a month left before official practices start. But over the next few weeks, the guys will slowly start filtering back into town, and a lot of them will join the practice session with us. It's the assholes who don't bother that we've got to worry about.

I let myself into my condo and lock my front door before I walk into the kitchen for a bottle of water.

"What the fuck?" Seriously.

What's with everyone being where they don't belong at four o'clock in the fucking morning today? "Why are you awake, B?" I ask my sister.

"Mommy called," she tells me from where she sits at my kitchen table, and I stop and grab the back of a chair.

My mind starts spinning worst-case scenarios. "Is everything okay? What happened?"

"Nobody calls in the middle of the night with good news, Ares. Daddy felt funny. He was having a hard time breathing. So they took him to the hospital."

I start to cut in, but she stops me with a look. "He's fine.

They did some scans. One of his stents needs to be replaced. They're doing it tomorrow. He'll be home the same day. But some guy in the ER recognized Dad. He knew he was the Wilder brothers' dad. Guess the media Mom and Dad got during the Stanley Cup finals really stuck. Anyway, she talked to Cross and was trying to get you. When she couldn't get you, she called me. She didn't want any of us to hear something on the news, if the guy went to the tabloids, and think it was worse than it actually is."

She pulls my phone from the pocket of the long sweater she has thrown over her pajamas. "Next time you sneak off to fuck Grace Sinclair, take your fucking phone."

"Watch your mouth, Bellamy," I warn her.

"Why are you hiding it? What the hell is wrong with you?"

"It's complicated," I admit. Because really . . . what else am I going to say?

"Do you care about her?" she asks, and I can't tell if she thinks I'm fucking this up or not.

"It's not that simple, B."

"It really is, A. You don't hide the people who matter. You stand next to them, loud and proud. If you've got to hide them, there's something wrong with your relationship." She stands and slams my phone against my chest. "And here's the thing, big brother. I know you. You're a pain in the ass. You're a serial procrastinator. And you're a shitty fucking cook. But you've got a heart of gold. And you refuse to lie. So from what I've seen this summer, I'm going to take a guess and say you're in love with good twin, and you're going along with what she wants. Because I'm pretty sure you wouldn't hide someone you love. What I can't figure out is why would *she*?"

She pats my chest where she just slammed my phone and takes a few steps before she turns back around. "She's making you a liar, A. You're a lot of things. But you're not a liar." With that, she disappears down the hall.

I make my way to my room, then drop on my bed and call my mom.

She answers right away, "Hey, Ares."

"Hey, Momma. I'm sorry I didn't answer when you called. I left my phone here when I went out earlier. You doing okay?"

"I'm okay, honey. Dad's gonna be okay too. Did Bellamy tell you that? I told her to make sure she didn't worry you. I'd be honest if it was a big deal."

"I know you would, Momma. I just felt like shit that you called and I missed it." I lie back and kick my shoes off. "How pissed is Dad?"

"Oh, he's pissed. It's outpatient surgery, but because we came in so late, they're making him stay the night. They were able to squeeze him in for tomorrow, but not until one in the afternoon."

"Ohh," I groan, remembering what a big, fat baby he was the last time he had surgery. "Can he eat before that?"

"Not a thing." She sighs.

"You gonna be in the room with him in the morning while he's bitching that he's hungry?"

"Oh, son. He's my husband. I'm not going to leave his side. Then when I bring him home tomorrow night, I'm going to torture him for days over what a baby he was. It's what marriage is all about."

We both get quiet for a minute. "You want to tell me where you were tonight without your phone?" she asks.

When I don't answer, she doesn't push.

"I hope she's a good girl, honey. You deserve a good girl."

I can feel my smile stretching. "She's a good girl, Mom. You'll love her."

"If you love her, I'll love her too, honey. Now go to bed.

I've got to get some sleep before I have to be back at the hospital tomorrow. I love you."

"Love you too, Momma." We end the call, and I close my eyes. I'm officially over this fucking night.

"Dude, pay attention," Cross yells across the ice, and my head snaps up just before Nixon steals the puck.

"Fuck."

"What the hell is your problem, Wilder?" Easton yanks his helmet off and squirts his water into his mouth. "You've been slow as shit out there today."

"Maybe he's cranky because he hasn't been sleeping in his own bed," Nixon offers up like a fucking little douchebag, and I fight the urge to tell him that's because I'm sleeping in his sister's bed.

An urge that's getting harder to fight, the longer Grace has been home.

And after my shit show of a night—*morning*—whatever the fuck it was—I'm thinking we're due for a discussion tonight.

"Whose bed you been sleeping in, Goldilocks?" Easton asks, and if I could skate off the ice without looking like a little bitch, I would. I'm too tired for this shit.

"I got a mom, and she lives in Maine, dude. Fuck off. I don't answer to you."

"Lunch at West End?" Cross offers up, and we all agree.

But when we're walking into the bar a few minutes later, my brother stops me. "You know Dad's gonna be fine, right?"

"Yeah, man. I know. Just got a lot on my mind."

"Like why you're sneaking out at night? Is everything okay, brother? Anything you need to talk to me about, I'm right here. No judgment," he tells me, like he's making any sense.

"What?" I stop and stare at him, not sure where he's going with this.

Cross shrugs and pushes the door open. "It's just not like you to be secretive about anything. I want to make sure you aren't getting into trouble. And honestly, you usually broadcast that shit too."

"Trouble?" I'm a grown man with a job, a mortgage, and people who depend on me. But this fucker is worried I'm getting into trouble.

And why is that?

Oh yeah. Because I'm lying about it, and he knows I'm hiding something.

"No trouble." I walk past him into the bar and hear him grumble behind me.

We walk over to where Nix and Easton are already sitting at the bar, and Nix closes his menu and hands it to me. "Come on, be honest. Is it a dude? Do you not want to tell us? Because seriously, we'd be cool."

I choke on my water as the bartender approaches us to take our orders, and I press my thumb and finger against my temple, way too fucking tired for this shit.

I wait for us all to order before I answer the morons, "It's not a dude. I'm not gay. No judgment if you are, Sinclair. But I like women."

"Fine. Then do we know her?" he pushes, and I swear to God, I'm gonna lose my shit. "Come on, man, I'm your best friend. Spill that shit."

"You're a grown man, shithead," I snap. "We don't have best friends."

"Dude. Don't hurt the kid's feelings," Cross tells me, and I stare back at him.

"Are you fucking with me, right now?" I ask my brother, then turn to Easton. "He's fucking with me, right?"

"Hey, man, I have enough family drama of my own. I'll leave you three to yours." Easton grins and drinks his beer.

"There's no family drama." Cross must see then that I'm over this shit because he changes the subject, and I decide maybe I need to be a little nicer to my brother. "Nix, what time does your mom want us at the house for dinner tonight?"

"I think she said six when I talked to her."

Easton passes our beers down the bar. "Nice to see it's not my wife's family demanding the big family shit for a change."

"Yeah well, I think she's just scared that Gracie's gonna get that job in Philly with that ballet company and she won't have too many of these left between football season, hockey season, and good twin leaving again."

My head snaps up, and I glare at Nix. "What are you talking about?"

"Mom got Grace an audition with the ballet she choreographs for in Philly. I heard Grace and Brynlee talking about it yesterday when I stopped by their place for dinner. Gracie's practicing today at Hart & Soul."

"You mean when you mooched food off your sister?" Cross asks him, but I tune out Nixon's answer.

And the hits just keep coming.

GRACE

If life's a walk in the park, I'm thinking mine is more like Jurassic Park and less like Central Park.
—*Grace's secret thoughts*

"Are you sure your foot isn't bothering you? Because your heart doesn't seem into this routine, Gracie."

Annabelle Sinclair is far from a stage mother. She never pushed me to live *her* dreams. But she is a dance teacher, and at the end of the day, I'm her student. Especially within the walls of Hart & Soul Academy of Dance. And as her student, she's always going to push me for more. To be *more*. To be perfect.

"Never forget, it's not just your spine you're trying to align, my girl. It's your soul. Dance so the world can see just how beautiful it is."

"Okay." I bend over and press my palms to my thighs. "I can do better."

"Can you?" Mom moves behind me, so we're standing

together in the mirror, and waits for me to straighten. Then she lifts my arms up, positioning them in Grande pose. "Because if this is too much, too fast, you don't have to take the audition." She adjusts the tilt of my head and smiles. "The stars will align again. If it's meant to be, it will be."

She slides her hands down to my hips and rests them there, happy with my form. "You have to believe that. The universe is a funny thing. And you might not be given what you want, but you're always given what you need."

She steps away, and I consider telling her to cancel the audition.

That's what Brynlee wanted.

She was furious when I told her I was taking it and hasn't spoken to me since.

But this doesn't hurt. Though it doesn't exactly feel good.

But I'm a professional. I can handle discomfort.

The bells above the front door of the studio chime. And as Mom steps out into the waiting room we call the fishbowl, I lift up onto my toes and balance in a beautiful arabesque.

I've always loved the lines of this position. But today, my muscles strain holding something I've been able to maintain easily for over a decade.

I stand in the center of my favorite of all of Mom's studios.

With it's gorgeous arched windows, white gauzy curtains, and beautiful natural lighting that filters in here, it's been my favorite place in the world for most of my life. My refuge when I needed to just dance through whatever problems I was having, this was the space I always ran to. But today . . . right now, it's the first time I feel like I'm running away instead of running to something.

"Honey." Mom steps into the room and looks at me through the reflection. "Ares is here, asking for you."

"Really?" *What the hell is he thinking?*

Mom nods but doesn't question me.

She's probably saving that for later. "I'm going to go grab lunch with Amelia at Sweet Temptations. Do you want anything?"

"No, thank you. I'll see you at your house tonight if I'm not here when you get back."

"Would you mind locking up? I'm not coming back. I need to grocery shop for dinner tonight. Daddy wants to grill ribs."

"Sure, Mom. Thanks." I follow her into the fishbowl and know right away Ares is pissed. But right about now, so am I.

"See you tonight, Annabelle," he tells her as she grabs her bag and walks out the front door.

I flip the sign to closed and lock the door behind my mom, then turn around. "What are you doing here?"

"What are *you* doing here?" His words are clipped and angry. And the way he looks at me isn't something I've ever seen from him before. It's cruel.

He stalks my way until I'm forced to take a few steps back. "When were you going to tell me you were auditioning for a new company?"

"I don't know," I tell him truthfully. "Tonight?" I answer, but I know I phrased it as a question for a reason. "It only just happened yesterday."

I don't lie to this man.

To myself. *Yes.*

To my family. *Possibly.*

To Ares. *Never.*

"Have you been cleared, good twin? Did Brynlee say you're okay to dance? Because you had your boot on two days ago when we were all at West End. You hadn't danced yet then. Or had you and you just *forgot* to tell me that too?"

"That's not fair," I attempt to defend myself because this is clearly an attack. But I'm not sure there's anything I can say that will make this better, and the fact that I'm already aware of that should be a flashing neon sign. "Today is the first time I've danced since we flew home from London."

"And why are you dancing today, Grace?" He moves into the studio and over to the sound system, where he pushes buttons until he finds a song he likes. "Your mom has great taste." And the way he says it holds an edge he's not bothering to hide.

"She does," I agree hesitantly.

"You gonna answer my question?" he pushes, and I want to scream, *No*.

Because he's not going to like any of my answers.

I'm not even sure I like any of my answers.

"What was I supposed to do? *Hmm*? My mom called in a favor to get me the audition. Was I supposed to skip it? *Thanks, but no thanks?* The world of ballet isn't that big, and I'm not Margot Fonteyn. I'm replaceable. Pretty sure Jenkins did it in an hour. I couldn't risk pissing off one more director." I take a tentative step toward him, and then another until we're toe-to-toe, and I touch him. The only thing . . . the only person who grounds me.

I press my palms against his chest and beg for him to understand. To see it my way. "She thought she was doing me a favor."

"Because"—his voice becomes harshly quiet—"you never told her how bad your injury was. Why are you so worried about disappointing someone that you'd risk your own health instead of being honest with them?"

"It's not like that," I argue, and he laughs, so damn angry.

"Tell me how it is, baby. Because I see you, even if you can't see yourself," he argues, so pissed he makes it easier for me to feel rage instead of guilt.

"I'm a professional. I'm at the top of my field. I know how

far I can push myself before I break. And I'm not breaking," I tell him, letting anger fuel me now.

"You're already broken, and you don't even see it, *do you*? When was the last time you did something you wanted to do, Grace? Something that was just for you?"

"I'm standing here with you. That's just for me. *You're just for me, god of war.*"

He makes a sound in the back of his throat, and a fiery fury burns behind his eyes. "Yeah. I guess I am, since you've been lying to everyone in your life about me anyway. Fuck, Grace. We're almost two months past London, and you're still not standing up for yourself. And what's worse is I'm letting you do it."

He holds my face in his hands and shakes his head as I stand, frozen in place. "Do you love me, Gracie? Because I'm so goddamned in love with you, I've lied to everyone I care about. For. You. I've snuck around like a fucking kid because it's what you asked. Because I love you."

He waits for an answer I'm so damn scared to give him.

Not because I don't feel it.

But because I don't know how to give him what he wants.

He's not asking me to put him first.

He's asking me to put myself first, and I don't know how to do that.

So I stand in front of him, silently begging for more time.

But Ares takes my silence as an answer in itself.

"Wow. I'm not sure how I missed it," he almost whispers. "Man, I guess I really am the idiot everyone thinks I am."

"You're not," I try to stop the accident happening in front of me, but it's so far past the point of collision, I'm practically standing on the sidelines watching someone uselessly perform CPR.

And because he's my god of war, he smiles a cold, calculated smile. "It's okay, Grace. What did you say in London? We never made each other any promises, right?"

"Ares . . ." I try to say more, but the words don't come.

"When's your audition, good twin?" He runs his hand up my neck, only it feels different. Indifferent. And I think that's worse than his anger.

"The end of the week," I whisper, and this man I love just shakes his head and presses his lips to my forehead before he steps back.

"Good luck."

I follow him out of the studio into the fishbowl and grab his hand. "Where are you going?"

"Up to Maine for a few days. I need to see my parents."

"Will you be at dinner tonight?" I ask, suddenly freaking out.

Ares stares at me for a long beat and then another.

"Good luck with your audition." And then he's gone, and I'm left standing alone.

I stand under the hot spray in the shower until the water turns icy cold, and even then, I don't move.

I can't.

Fear is my driving force, and it's crippling.

When my legs finally give out, and my sobs grow quiet in my raw throat, I turn off the water and slide to the shower floor, unable to move or care.

I'm not sure what's worse.

Knowing you're fucking up and being unable to stop yourself, or hurting the person who means everything and watching them walk away, knowing it was your fault.

They're both pretty damn bad.

Brynlee pounds on my bathroom door. "I know you're alive in there because the water shut off. Now get your ass out here."

Damn it.

I force myself up and throw on my robe before I open the door and find an incredibly pissed-off Brynn in my bedroom. "Brynn . . . I can't do this right now."

"Well, I don't actually give a single shit what you think you can and can't do *right now*, good twin. How long have we known each other?"

"Brynnie . . ."

"Twenty years. It's been twenty years since you and Everly walked up to me in ballet class and asked if I liked chocolate milk or strawberry milk. Twenty years. That's a long time," she yells, and I cringe, not sure that this is any better than her freezing me out yesterday.

"I know Evie is your sister, but I love you like a sister, and I refuse to stand by and watch you fuck up your life."

I open my mouth, and she glares. "I need you to hear me out. Because I'm aware that you know your body, but I'm the one who spent five and a half years in school to get my doctorate, and I've been working with elite fucking athletes for three years since. And don't forget the years spent in school, working on the fighters at Dad's gym. I know an athlete's body, Grace. And you might be fine for your audition. But you aren't fine to go back to dancing seven days a week for ten hours a day just yet. You will be. But you need more time."

I stand there and take it. Every word of it. Until I'm sure she's gotten it all off her chest.

"I've got to take this audition, Brynn."

She presses her lips together, disappointment hanging thick between us. "I know you think that, Grace. But at some point in your life, you're going to have to ask yourself if you're dancing for you or because that's what everyone expects you to do."

She shakes her head, frustrated, like it's so obvious . . . such an easy thing to change.

"I don't think you're going to like the answer."

When I don't say anything else, she shakes her head. "You're still going, aren't you?"

I don't have to say anything.

She already knows my answer.

"Yeah. That's what I thought."

ARES

I'm already awake when my mom knocks on my door the morning after I fly in.

Not sure if I'm sober.

But I'm awake.

When I got in last night, Dad was already in bed, and Mom was dozing on the couch. She yelled at me for coming. Said I didn't need to upend my life for them. I didn't have the heart to tell her my life had already been upended. Instead, I locked up after she went to bed and broke out the bottle of shitty old scotch Cross and I had hidden in the basement over a decade ago and decided to crack it open.

That's a decision I'll be paying for today.

Shitty booze leaves you with a shittier hangover.

I knew it but didn't care enough to not drink it anyway.

Gracie is numb, so I figured I'd give it a shot and see if that works for me.

News flash. Booze might numb the pain, but it magnifies the problem. At least for me it did. Can't say I felt like a winner sitting in my parents' kitchen, drinking cheap scotch from a coffee mug, wishing things were different.

Not exactly a highlight.

A low point . . . Maybe.

But in all fairness, I've done worse.

Just haven't felt worse in a long damn time.

"Ares," Mom calls out from the other side of the door. "There's coffee."

Very, very, very fucking slowly, I get up from my old twin bed and answer my bedroom door. "Thanks, Mom. I've got to take a shower. Then I'll be down."

"Oh, sweetie." She wrinkles her nose and takes a step back. "You smell like a distillery."

"Thanks, Ma."

"Your father is having coffee on the porch. He shouldn't need anything. I'm going into town to run a few errands. Do you need anything? Maybe some new shampoo? Deodorant?"

"Very funny. No, I'm good. I've got that stuff. Nothing a hot shower and some strong coffee won't fix." At least what can be fixed.

"You going to tell me what's hurting you, honey? I hope it's not worry over your father because he's as strong as a bull. You don't need to worry about him." She reaches out to run her hand over my head, then changes her mind. I must look like flaming dog shit—or worse.

"Just wanted to see you guys. I didn't like the call the other night, and we don't get back up here enough." I drop a kiss on her cheek, and she smiles, but it doesn't reach her eyes.

"If that's what you say." She lightly taps my cheek, then wipes her hand on my t-shirt.

I'll be back in a little while. Go shower. And don't let your father talk you into making bacon." She turns to leave, mumbling something under her breath about stupid, stubborn men, and I'm pretty sure she's talking about Pop and me.

I lift my arm to close the door and get a whiff of myself.

Shit. I *am* ripe.

Shower first. Coffee after.

I've got this.

I turn to grab my dopp kit and trip over my sneakers, suddenly less sure of my level of gotting this. *Getting this* . . . Having this. Yeah. Having this.

Fuck. I think I'm still drunk.

A hot shower and a fresh shave help enough that I no longer feel the alcohol seeping out of my pours. Swear to God, I've lost my touch. I didn't even finish the bottle. There was a time I would have said that move was for quitters and I'm no quitter. Now I quit three-quarters of the way through, and I still feel like fucking ass.

I make my way into the kitchen and pour myself a cup of black coffee before I go searching for Dad. Not that it's a long search. He's right where Mom said he'd be—on the porch. Their house sits on top of a hill in Kennebunkport, Maine. It's not huge, but the view . . . You can't beat it. The ocean waves beat against the shore below. The boats dock in the distance, and the salt air reminds you you're alive. Pretty sure it's Dad's favorite thing in the world, after Mom, Bellamy, and the grandkids. Cross and I tie for last, but I'm okay with that.

"Hey, old man." I walk through the squeaky screen door and sit down in the rocker next to his. "How are you feeling?"

"I'm fine, you idiot. You didn't need to come all the way

up here to check on me." He watches me sit and drinks his coffee. "Unless you had a different reason for coming. Saw the scotch on the counter, kid. And a man doesn't drink like that by himself if it ain't about a woman."

I look away and drink my coffee quietly.

But Dad's move is usually to wait us out.

Mom can't stand the not talking.

Dad doesn't give a shit. He's in no rush.

"Might have been a little of both," I finally tell him as I watch a fishing boat pulling into the harbor. "But can we not tell Mom?"

"I don't know anything," he agrees. "Now what's brought you up here, Ares?"

This time, I do turn and look at him. "Seriously, old man. You had open heart surgery yesterday. Do I need a better reason?"

"And I always thought Bellamy was the drama queen. Jesus Christ, kid. It wasn't open heart surgery. They went through a vein and cleaned out a stent. I'm fine. Now, what's your real reason?"

"Fine, you old fucker. It's a girl."

Dad smiles and puts his coffee cup down. "Now we're getting to the real reason. Who's the girl?"

"Don't bother asking. I'm not telling," I grumble.

"So, it's a girl we know. Son, you better not be messing around with the girl Bellamy brought home with her when school let out last May. I did some digging after she stayed here. Do you know who her father is?"

"Caitlin?"

Dad nods, and I fucking laugh. "She and Bellamy have been sharing a room at my place while they look for a place of their own. And no, it's not Caitlin."

"Is it one of those girls your brother's wife is friends with? They're all pretty. That one is going to be a doctor. You could do worse, Ares." He's fucking serious. What the fuck? This is why I don't talk about women with my dad.

"Jesus, Dad. It's none of them, okay?" I stand up and lean against the wooden porch railing, then turn back to face him and cross my ankles. "If you repeat this, I'll never tell you another thing as long as I live, Pop."

His eyes light up like a gossipy girl, and I want to laugh, but it would just piss him off.

"I've been seeing Grace."

"Grace who?" he asks, and he's dead serious.

"What do you mean, Grace who? Everly's twin sister, Grace."

His face twists like he needs to piece together what I'm saying. "The ballerina?"

"Yeah. The ballerina. We started talking last year, and things got serious after the season." Well, that's the short version of the long and short of it.

"I thought she lived in Paris or some place like that . . ." he mumbles, still trying to figure something out. Not sure what though.

"She did. But she came home with me a few months ago. She hurt herself and needed to rehab at home before she figured out what she was doing." My anger simmers as I start replaying our fight over in my mind.

"Well, what's the problem then? You don't want to do long distance? I mean, it's a legitimate concern, but probably one you should have thought of before you started dating your brother's sister-in-law. Wait—isn't her brother living with you?"

"Yeah. That's part of the problem. Her family. She wanted us to keep things quiet. She wasn't ready for everyone to know and get involved. Grace is a real people pleaser—"

He interrupts me, "There are worse things to be than someone who wants people to be happy."

"What about if she's hurting herself in the process?" I mull over my next words before I say them. Pretty sure they're gonna make me sound like a girl. "What if it hurts me?"

"Do you love her, Ares?"

One simple question with no simple answer.

"It's complicated."

"And . . ." Dad pushes back, and I give in.

"Yeah. I do."

"Then the answer is simple. I named you after the goddamned god of war . . . You fight for her. Because there is nothing more important in the entire world than love. The love of a good woman. The love a father has for his children and grandchildren. It's why I wake up every day and why I say a prayer before I go to bed every night. Fight for it the way you've fought for everything you've ever wanted your entire life. It was all leading to this."

"I don't know, Pop. I'm not sure she feels the same way," I admit, knowing I asked her point blank yesterday and she didn't answer. "I think there comes a time when you have to walk away from a fight if that person isn't willing to fight for themselves or you."

"That's the stupidest thing I ever heard. But you've always been stubborn and needed to learn things the hard way. So you do what you feel like you've got to do. But try to keep an open mind, and don't wait too long, Ares. Life waits for no man." He stands a little slower than normal and grabs our mugs. "Now. With that in mind, what do you say you make us some bacon, egg, and cheese sandwiches."

"Mom said no bacon, Pops. It clogs your arteries." I open the door and wait for him to walk through. How about an egg white omelet?" I ignore him grumbling and head to the kitchen. He told me to fight. Might as well pick this as my first hill to stand on.

GRACE

⟨⟨⟩⟩

> GRACE
> I miss you.

He leaves me on read again, and I fight the urge to cry as I stare at my phone.

It's been days, and I haven't heard a word from him. The only reason I even know he's still in Maine is because Nixon mentioned it this morning when he stopped by.

> GRACE
> Nix told me your dad is doing good and that you guys went fishing. Hope you caught a big one.

I start and stop a million messages, but in the end, I delete them all and close out of my texts. I've got an audition to stretch for.

I'm a ball of tangled nerves as I step on the grand stage of one of the oldest ballet companies in the country. The Philadelphia City Ballet may be less prestigious than The Royal Ballet or the New York City Ballet, but there are few others in the world that can hold a candle to the tradition of beauty they're steeped in. Though, as I take center stage and wait for the music to begin, I can't help but wonder if the nerves are hitting so hard because I'm nervous I won't get the part or I'm terrified that I will.

"Thank you for coming in to audition for us today, Ms. Sinclair." The artistic director calls out from third row center, where he's flanked by who I'm guessing is the assistant artistic director and possibly a board member. They sit in a tight pod, prepared to dissect my every move.

"We are very big fans of your mother and appreciate her letting us know that someone of your caliber with your family history was currently available. A bit unusual though. Would you mind telling us why you're no longer with The Royal Ballet?"

"I needed to take time to rehab an injury, and in doing so, I realized how much I missed being home. As you're well aware, Philadelphia is my home. This is the company I grew up dreaming of." I wait, hoping they don't see my unease and relax slightly when they smile.

"Very good, Ms. Sinclair. Let's get started, shall we?" He nods toward the wings where I'm sure my music is being queued up, and I slide into place, prepared to give the performance of a lifetime.

"Brynn... how long are you going to ignore me?" I ask as I plop down next to her on the couch with a bowl of ice cream for each of us.

Yup.

I'm resorting to bribery.

"Brynnie, it's been over a week." I hold the strawberry ice cream with chocolate syrup and diced-up strawberries covered in whipped cream out in front of her face and slide it back and forth under her nose. "I got your favorite from the new ice creamery on Main Street. They make it fresh."

Then I give up and take a big spoonful of the deliciousness and moan. "Come on, Brynn. It's so good."

Finally, she pushes her glasses on top of her head and looks up from her laptop at me. "You can't buy your way out of this with ice cream, Grace. Not this time. Did you take the job?"

"They haven't offered it to me yet."

She grabs the ice cream off the table and moans around a spoonful. "Fuck. That is good. But you and me . . ." She moves the spoon between the two of us. "Yeah . . . We're not good. Not yet, Grace. I'm still mad at you. And I don't know how long it's going to take me to get over it. Even ice cream can't fix this." She picks up her bowl and her MacBook and marches down the hall, then slams her bedroom door.

Well... damn.

I sit, trying to figure out how I got here, what I did that was the catalyst.

And the scary thing is I can't pinpoint any one thing. I know what I did to upset Brynlee, and I know exactly how I broke Ares's heart. But the catalyst—the original one—would have come long before that.

Fuck this.

I grab my bowl, the carton of ice cream, and my keys, then storm out of the apartment, enjoying the sound of the door slamming behind me. Two can play this game, and I can be just as loud.

I march over to the elevator and hit the up button, seeing Bellamy peek out of her door. "What's got your panties in a twist, good twin?"

When I turn around and glare at her, she takes a step back. "Oh shit. Good twin is pissed. Do I need to get your brother?"

"No. But if your brother comes home, let me know." The elevator doors open, and I step inside, a woman on a mission.

A minute later, I'm even more worked up and pounding on the penthouse door. "Maddox . . . Callen . . . One of you had better be home."

"Damn, good twin. You've got a fucking key. Stop making so much noise. I spent the day in training camp and having your father chew your ass out in front of your entire team is fucking exhausting."

I shove the carton of ice cream into Callen's hands.

"Is Madman here?" I move to the stairs and call up, "Maddox. Get your ass down here."

"Holy shit, Gracie." Killian St. James comes out of the bathroom and smiles. "I haven't seen you in forever."

"Yeah well, your sister pissed me off. So right now, you're guilty by association. Bye bye, Killer."

Callen all but chokes on the ice cream the fucker is eating right out of the carton, and I point my spoon at him. "Wrong answer, Callen."

Maddox comes down the stairs just as Killian is heading

toward his room and stops to warn him, "Dude, run . . . Something fucking snapped, and good twin has gone psycho."

Maddox watches him, unamused. "What the hell, Gracie? What's going on?"

I pace with the ice cream in my hand until I finally move over to the dining room table and sit my ass down on top of it with my legs swinging. "I need you to be brutally honest with me."

"You've got a great ass, Grace." Maddox crosses his arms and waits with a smug fucking smile, like he just solved world hunger.

"I know I have a great ass, shithead. I don't need you to tell me I'm pretty. I need you to help me get unbroken." Even saying the words feels strangely cathartic and equally paralyzing.

"I'm out." Callen hands Maddox the ice cream, and Maddox shoves him back.

"Man the fuck up, asshole." And when he turns to me, the look on his face says so many things I'm not sure I could have ever heard from anyone else.

"You're not broken, Grace." Callen watches Maddox as he navigates the bomb I just dropped at his feet and sits down on the dining room table next to me.

"Fucker, that can't hold your heavy ass," Maddox groans. "Get the hell off before you break it."

"Dude. Do you know how many times I've bent someone over this table?" Callen argues, and I gag and carefully move off it.

Maddox shakes his head, utterly embarrassed for my manwhore uncle. "Over it, asshole. Not both of you on it."

"I've—"

"I'm begging you," I stop him. "Please don't. Only one Sinclair can be psychoanalyzed at a time. And right now, it's my turn." I look between the two of them and sigh. I trust both these men with my life. Truly. Completely. And it still hurts to say what I need to say. "Do you think I'm . . . I mean . . . Do you remember . . . ?"

I want to scream and cry and rip my hair out by the roots, I'm so frustrated.

How did I get here?

Finally, I just spit it out.

"Have I ever had a backbone?"

"The fuck?" Callen asks, not following my train of thought at all.

Not that I can blame him.

But Madman . . . His eyes are locked on me, and what I see shining back isn't pretty.

"You want brutal honesty, good twin?" He takes my empty bowl from my hands and hands me the half-full carton of ice cream. "You sure you're really ready for it?"

"No, I'm not ready. But I'm twenty-five, and I've always been treated like spun glass that could shatter at any moment. And if I don't figure out my life soon, I'm going to lose things . . . I'm going to lose people I'm not willing to lose. But for me to fight those fucking battles, I've got to figure out the other ones first."

"You've always been more worried about everyone else's feelings than your own, Grace. Christ." Callen runs his hands over his buzzed head. "You made sure you had Oreos for your snack every day at school because my mom refused to pack them for me. And you wanted me to have the snack I wanted, even if it meant you didn't have one because no first grader wants carrots and ranch as a snack. You're a people pleaser. You're a giver. What's wrong with that?"

"You were so sad when your mom said you couldn't have those stupid cookies." I laugh as my eyes start to well up. "I can still remember the way you smiled when I gave you mine. I loved that I made you smile."

"That, right there, is the problem, Gracie." Maddox steers me over to their giant black sectional sofa.

This room used to be so pretty and feminine.

Now it looks like a stripper should be standing on the coffee table.

But hey, one thing at a time.

"You have the biggest heart, but man, good twin, you're the first one to do everything for everyone else. I don't remember the last time you did something for yourself. I thought maybe you were going to when you came home from London. But from what I heard, you changed your mind."

"What are you talking about?" My eyes burn as we get deeper into this. Because I don't care how self-aware you are, having someone point out your flaws to your face feels like your skin has been flayed open and you're being dipped in acid.

"How many times did I visit you in London?" Madman asks with a softer smile than I've ever seen him give anyone but his mother.

"Three. But I thought that was because you were banging Lennon."

"Okay. Well that too, but I came for you. Because the first time I came in February, you were so miserable, it fucking scared me." He sits down on the coffee table across from me and holds my gaze. "Yeah, you were smiling. But it was forced. It was always forced. At least until you came home. Then it got more real again."

"Why didn't you say anything?" I ask softly, scared to go deeper.

Scared to open myself up to more.

"Because you're a grown woman. Even if everyone treats

you like they know what you want and need better than you do, only you can let them. And only you can stop them. Your acceptance was your permission."

I suck in a breath like I'd just been dropped from the highest lift in front of the biggest audience I've ever danced for. My hands move to my stomach, and I have to force the air out of my lungs. "How did you see that if I couldn't?"

Callen sits down next to me and takes my hand in his.

Offering me his silent strength.

"Not knowing something and choosing to ignore it are two completely different things, Gracie." Maddox sits down on my other side and wraps his arms around my shoulder.

"Do you even like dancing, good twin?" Callen squeezes my hand between his, and the first tear falls. "Or do you just do it because you're good at it and your mom and Evie say you need to dance? Because I don't think they know you don't want to do it anymore, but I'm pretty sure you don't."

"How?" I ask so quietly the word barely leaves my lips.

"I might not be the most observant guy, but I know a thing or two about following in family footsteps. And I've had to fight to do it every step of the way. You . . . you're a fucking natural. I'm a dude. We don't like ballet. Anyone who says they do is trying to fuck you. Remember that."

"Get to the point, asshole," Maddox tells Callen as I absorb another shock to my soul.

"I love watching you dance. My point is everyone loves watching you dance so damn much, I don't think any of us ever realized you didn't want to do it anymore. You're not me. You're not fighting for it. You're giving in to it because you want the little fat kid who shouldn't have Oreos to smile."

"Jesus Christ, Cal," Maddox groans.

But not me.

I turn to him—this man who has only lived on this earth

for five days without Evie and me—and throw my arms around him. "You should always smile, Callen. You have a great smile."

He wraps his big arms around me and squeezes. "We can't tell you what to do, Gracie. If we do, we're as bad as everyone else."

I shake my head. "They're not bad because I never told them either. I've spent so much of my life being afraid of disappointing everyone that I didn't see what was right in front of my face . . ." I swallow down my overwhelming emotion and stand up. "I was making them happy by making myself miserable. And they're all going to be so mad when they find out."

Maddox stands up and hands me the now-melted ice cream. "What are you going to do now?"

"I'm not sure, but I'll have time to figure it out while I find a job."

GRACE

You have to love yourself, before you can love someone else.
—Grace's secret thoughts

"She's been like this for days." Brynn's voice bounces around in my mind, like a bad dream I can't wake up from.

"What do you want me to do about it?" Okay, why the fuck is Maddox in my dream?

I yank the blanket over my head and try to tune them out.

"I don't know. Fix it." Dream Brynn sounds annoyed. But bonus points—if she's annoyed, she still cares, right?

"Why me?" Madman sounds scared. That's weird. Nothing scares him.

"Because I'm not talking to her, and I can't call Everly. You're neutral, and Killian said she came to the penthouse the other night all fired up. Whatever you said to her broke

Gracie. And I really don't want to have to tell her sister that good twin broke on my watch."

Fuck this shit.

I throw my blanket off my head and glare at the two of them.

"Oh, Gracie . . . When was the last time you showered?" Brynn momentarily forgets she's not speaking to me to personal-hygiene shame me. Got it.

"She didn't look like that when she left the penthouse the other night," Maddox defends himself. I look from him to Brynn, then back to him where I can fixate on the Sweet Temptations coffee cup in his hand.

I sit up, and they both back up like they're about to be attacked by a zombie from *The Walking Dead*. Shit. How many new Negan episodes did I miss? Whatever. I grab the coffee cup from Maddox and take my first sip of anything besides water in two days.

"I'm sick, you assholes." No sooner have the words left my mouth than I run to the bathroom and dry heave because there's absolutely nothing left in my empty stomach.

Maddox's voice filters in, but I've got no clue what he's saying.

Brynlee, however, walks in, runs cool water over a washcloth, and runs it over my forehead before she lifts my hair and lays it over the back of my neck. "Have you been running a fever too?"

"Like you care," I manage to whisper pitifully between heaves that leave my stomach even emptier than it already was.

"That's not fair, Gracie. I'm allowed to be mad at you and disagree with you and still care." She grabs a hair tie from the counter and pulls my hair back, then moves around the bathroom and turns the water on in the tub before she leaves me alone.

I curl up on the floor, lacking the energy or will to move.

I close my eyes and just want this shitty week to be over already.

"Come on." Brynn's hands force me up and into the tub.

"I'm in pajamas," I croak.

"They're booty shorts and a tank top with puke stains. They'll survive, and when they do, we'll burn them."

I lean my head against the wall and close my eyes. "Is Ares back from Maine yet?"

When she doesn't answer, I force my eyes back open and see the answer on her face. "Oh."

"Have you tried calling him?"

I'd probably cry if I had any fluid left for my body to expel.

Reading my mind, she cracks open a bottle of water and hands it to me. "Tiny sips, Grace." She takes it back from me once I stop and sits it on the edge of the tub. "He's been home for a few days."

"Oh." It's all I've got in me.

"Lift your arms, sweetie. I changed my mind. You need to get out of this shirt."

I don't bother arguing and lift my arms as far as I can, then wrap them around my knees.

Brynn takes the hand shower wand and washes my hair, then rinses off my body.

Everything hurts. My head. My heart. My body.

"I decided not to take the job," I whisper. And she stops what she was doing. Shocked.

"Really? You turned them down?"

I nod without opening my eyes. "I don't want to dance anymore."

"When was the last time you wanted to dance, Grace?"

Why did she have to ask me that?

"Honestly . . . I don't remember."

Brynn unplugs the tub and grabs me a towel. "Why don't you dry off, and I'll change your sheets."

"Brynnie . . . *I'm sorry.* I'm sorry I didn't listen to you. I'm sorry I took you for granted. I'm sorry for everything. I promise to take better care of myself. Please don't be mad at me anymore. I promise I'm trying. But I might need your help," I practically plead, so damn tired of not having my best friend.

She wraps the warm towel around me and helps me stand. "We might have loves of our lives out there waiting for us, Gracie. But the five of us—me, you, Evie, Lindy, and Kenzie—we're soulmates. We'll always have your back. I'll always want what's best for you. But I'm done standing by and watching you hurt yourself. So you better be good with tough love."

I rest my head on her shoulder and stand, dripping on the tile floor. "Can we start tough love when I don't feel like I'm dying?"

"How about we wait until you no longer look like you've got chicken pox from all the broken capillaries on your face? Seriously, how much have you thrown up?"

"It's been days," I croak out and reach for the water to take another sip.

"I'm sorry. If I were here, I'd have known."

"Where were you?"

"That's a whole other story."

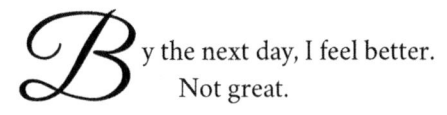

By the next day, I feel better.
Not great.

But better.

Brynn got enough water, ginger ale, and chicken soup in me to help me at least feel more human again. Then she threw me in shorts and a t-shirt, put slippers on my feet, and told me we were going outside. "Come on. It's beautiful out. You need some vitamin D."

"I'm not ready to see anyone yet. I've got to prep myself to talk to Mom and Evie before I can tell them I turned down the job." I know it's coming. I know I need to talk to them about that. About Ares. About all the important things in my life, but a little more energy would be good for that conversation.

"I know. We're just going to sit on the roof deck and get you some sun. You still look gray, good twin."

I still feel gray too. But I don't tell her that as I grab my sunglasses from my purse and follow her out the door. We walk by Ares's door, and I wish I could just knock on it. I want to fix things between us more than anything in the world. But he deserves someone who's being honest in his life. And that's not me.

Not yet.

It's going to be me very soon. And once that's done . . . Well, I just hope it's not too late.

She hits the elevator button just as the door opens, and my heart sinks into my stomach.

Ares, Bellamy, Nixon, and Caitlin all pile off the elevator.

My God, he looks good.

So good . . . I could cry right here over the way my heart hurts seeing him.

I've called.

I've texted.

He's ignored it all. Not that I blame him, but to see him now looking so happy . . . Happy and sexy as fuck with the damn backward baseball hat. And here I am, looking like something the cat dragged in, if we had a damn cat.

I watch him take another step before Caitlin hops on his back for a piggyback ride. And I want to rip her eyes out of her head for the way she's looking at him. Touching him when I can't. Like she belongs there.

He doesn't even look at me, and I'm not sure which hurts worse.

His anger before or his lack of it now.

Ares

We walk into the condo, and I drop Caitlin's feet to the floor. "What the hell was that?"

"Oh, don't act like Grace Sinclair wasn't looking at you all doe-eyed. Let her see you having fun."

I look around to see if Nixon has come in yet, but he probably stopped to talk to Grace.

"Don't be a bitch, Cait."

She rolls her eyes, not listening to a word I say. Caitlin doesn't listen to anyone. "Whatever, dude. Your girl did you dirty or you wouldn't have run off to Maine and certainly wouldn't have slept in your bed every night since you came back."

Like I don't fucking know Grace screwed me. Like I'm not the one pissed off at her and myself because it's not like her sucking at the whole relationship thing makes me love her less.

"Fuck you. You don't know anything." I walk away from

her and into my room, where I shut the door, not willing to have this conversation.

Not now, and sure as hell not with her.

Bellamy knocks on my door a few minutes later, then pops her head in. "Can I come in?"

"You're basically in already, B. What's up?"

"Nix just said Grace's been sick. Nasty flu." She leans against the door and watches for a reaction. "Thought you might want to know."

"Does everyone know about us?" I ask her, too tired of this shit to even care who does and doesn't know anymore. If it wouldn't hurt Grace if Nixon found out, I'd tell him myself.

"No." She walks inside and shuts the door behind herself. "Nixon is oblivious. So are Cross and Everly. But you guys didn't do the greatest job of hiding what was happening. More so her than you."

"What?" I press, genuinely unsure of what she's trying to say.

"Grace Sinclair couldn't keep her eyes off you. Whenever we'd all hang out, she always made sure there was cherry coke and pepperoni pizza. You have the tastebuds of a child, by the way."

"What does any of that have to do with me?"

"The girl would make sure you had the food you liked, Ares. The drink you liked. Girls don't do that if they don't care. Especially girls who don't eat or drink that shit. And your girl only strays from rabbit food for chocolate or ice cream. Trust me, I've watched. I might not have liked that you two were keeping your shit quiet. But I did like how happy you were. And I kinda feel like me giving you shit that morning may have played into whatever happened between you two."

"It didn't have anything to do with you, B. I promise."

This shitstorm was all on us.

Bellamy leaves, and I look at my phone and scroll through her messages.

> GRACE
> I miss you.

It's dated from almost a week ago.

I didn't answer her then, and I'm not going to answer now.

But fuck . . . I want to.

I reach for my phone without opening my eyes.

Who the fuck calls in the middle of the night?

What time is it?

I squint and look at the screen. It's after four in the morning.

And shit.

"Hello," I answer as soon as I see it's Mom.

"Ares . . ." she cries.

"Mom, what's wrong?"

"Oh, honey. I didn't know who to call first. It's Dad."

I sit up, and the world stops spinning around me. "What's wrong, Mom? What do you need?"

"Oh, Ares. He's gone . . ." she sobs, and I stare at my phone in shock and denial.

I just saw him a week ago.

He can't be gone.

He was fine.

He was talking and smiling and trying to get me to sneak him bacon and bourbon.

He was telling me life was too damn short.

And now... "He's gone."

GRACE

Today is a new day, and I'm living my life. Not as the little girl afraid of flames, but as the woman who's walked through fire.
—*Grace's secret thoughts*

I can do this. I look at myself in the bathroom mirror, completely disgusted that I still feel like shit. But at least I'm satisfied with the makeup I've applied to look less walking-dead-*ish*.

I refuse to let Ares Wilder walk by me again like I don't exist, probably thinking he means nothing to me, when he means everything. I'm going to tell him how much I love him and beg him to give me just a few more days to get my shit together and deal with my family. I was going to talk to them first, but then I realized it was stupid to wait. He's my priority.

I'll scream it from the top of Kings Stadium, for all I care.

Wow. I really suck at pep talks.

But I'm going to give it a try anyway.

I fluff my hair, fix my boobs, and think about spritzing my favorite body spray, but considering I'm still not feeling great, I'm gonna have to forgo that one.

"You look cute," Brynn tells me as she pours coffee in her to-go cup. "You got a hot date?"

"I'm going to try to talk to Ares before he meets the guys for ice time today."

Brynlee looks slightly impressed. "What about Nixon?"

"It's about time I dealt with my family. He'll probably be one of the easier ones to handle, so fuck 'em."

"Vicious, good twin. I like it. Good luck."

Not really vicious. More like so unbelievably fried that my give-a-fuck meter just might be irrevocably broken.

"Thanks, Brynnie." I grab my keys and phone and stuff them in the pocket of my maxi dress, then head down the hall and knock on Ares's door.

Jesus. This man knows how I taste.

Why am I so nervous that I think I'm going to be sick again?

When the door opens, it's Caitlin—not Ares—on the other side, and I guess I'm still not over her twatty little move from yesterday because I walk right past her into the condo. "Is Ares in his room?"

"Shit. You don't know?" she asks, and genuine concern seems to have replaced whatever thought she was having a moment ago.

"Know what?" I ask very carefully, not liking the sound of this at all. "Where's Nixon? Is everyone okay?"

"Hey, good twin." Nix walks into the room with a bottle of vitamin water in his hand. "You okay? You're looking kinda . . . green."

"What don't I know?" I ask them both as the nausea

grows. "Where's Ares? Where is he?" I reach out for Nixon. "Is he all right?"

"He's fine, Grace. But his dad died last night. They all flew up there first thing this morning. Everly and the kids too. She probably hasn't had a chance to call yet."

I freeze for a moment, thinking of how Ares must be feeling, but then find the only word that comes into my mind. "No."

I reach for the chair to steady myself as the room starts to spin. "I've got to . . . I gotta go."

I turn for the door, and Nixon follows me down to my condo. "Let me come with you, Grace."

"I'm fine, Nix. I just can't shake the flu, and I'm going to be sick." I push through my front door and head straight to the bathroom, not bothering to shut the door.

A minute later, Brynn walks in with another wet washcloth. "You need to make a doctor's appointment. What if this is something else? A new strain of something? They might be able to give you antibiotics."

I wipe my mouth and sit back on my ass. "I've got to get to Maine, Brynn. Ares's dad died. I've got to get to him."

"Oh, Gracie. That's horrible. But okay—let me take you to the urgent care first, then to the airport. Let them give you a scrip you can take with you. You don't want to be puking on the plane."

If I'd been honest about Ares from the get-go, he'd have been in my bed last night when he got the call. I would have been there for him, helping him through this instead of finding out hours later.

"Come on, good twin." Brush your teeth and pack your bag."

"Thank you," I tell her, surprised I'm able to stand under the heavy weight of my guilt. "I appreciate it."

"What do you want me to tell Nix?"

I look at her for a minute and realize just how much time I've wasted trying to please other people before I call out my brother's name. Guess it's time to pull up the big-girl panties and deal with this.

He walks into my bedroom as I pull my suitcase from my closet. "You feeling better?"

"Listen. I've been seeing Ares all summer. Really, if I'm honest with myself, I've been with him since Everly's wedding last December. Now you know. Tell Mom and Dad or don't tell them. I'll deal with the fallout after we get through the funeral."

"What?" He looks at me like I just spoke gibberish.

"Oh wait." I turn back around. "I also quit ballet. There, that should be everything for now." I feel strangely liberated. Still kinda queasy, but that doesn't have anything to do with finally setting my secrets free. I think this is growth, but it's all a little too raw and overwhelming to analyze right now.

"Seriously?" he asks with a dopey grin. "You've been the dude?"

This time it's my turn to be the one confused. "What?"

"You're whose bed goldilocks has been sleeping in," Nixon answers like that makes more sense.

"Listen to me very carefully, Nix." I start stuffing clothes in my little, rolling carry-on suitcase. "I'm sick. I'm probably still dehydrated. I've lost seven pounds in four days, and I've slept like shit since Ares and I got into a fight almost two weeks ago. I need to get some medicine and a ticket for a flight to Maine. If you can help me with any of those, awesome. If not, I'll see you when I get home in a few days."

Damn. I really should have tried not giving a shit what anyone else thought years ago.

This is definitely underrated.

Of course, I'm telling the family member least likely to freak the fuck out. But still—

"I guess get your bag packed then, and I'll book your flight for you." He starts to walk away but stops before he gets far. "Grace . . . Is he good to you?"

I hold back the crazy current of tears threatening to drag me under. "He's the only person in the world who I've ever felt like I could be myself with, Nix. He's the best man I've ever known. And with any luck, he's forgiving too—because he deserved to be loved so much better than I made him feel."

"You love him?" Nix asks with a crooked smile.

"More than anything in this world," I tell him without hesitation, and my God, it feels good to finally admit that to someone.

Nix shakes his head. "Okay, then. I'll book us flights up there. You pack your bag."

"Us?" I ask, trying desperately to get my stuff together.

"I'm not letting my sick sister fly to Maine alone. What if something happens to you?"

"You don't have to do that, Nixon. I've got this." And I really do.

Point one for the new Gracie.

"I know I don't *have to*, good twin. But that's what family does. Am I booking the earliest tickets I can get?"

I love my brother. "I've got to swing by urgent care first."

"Got it. Now, hurry up while I do this. Pack."

"Thanks, Nix. I appreciate it." And I do appreciate him doing this for me, but I also appreciate that he asked me what I wanted.

Baby steps.

Ares

The sun is setting by the time we get through everything that needs to be handled for the day. We made the funeral arrangements, ordered the flowers, and picked out an urn. It's been a long day, and Mom handled it better than us. And at the end of it all, I find her sitting in Dad's rocker on the porch, staring out over the view that used to bring him so much joy.

"Hey, Momma."

She watches me sit down in the chair I was just in last week, talking to Dad about life and love, and my heart fucking hurts, thinking about it all now. "How's everyone doing inside?"

"Cross and Everly are putting the kids to bed, and Bellamy is baking banana bread."

"Good," Mom muses, always the rock of the family. Even today. "He'd hate that we're having a big service."

"It's not a big service, Mom."

"Anything bigger than me, you, your brother, and sister would be too big for him. Well, and Everly and the kids." She smiles when she thinks about the grandkids, and there goes my heart again.

He'll never get to know my kids or my wife one day.

"Your father was proud of the man you've grown into, Ares. You like to fly under the radar, but he saw you. We both do . . . *did*. He was so happy he got to spend time with you last week."

Words fail me, and I nod and get lost as I watch the boats in the harbor.

"Ares . . . Isn't that Everly's sister? When did she dye her hair?"

I look up and see Grace getting out of an Uber, and my heart pangs seeing her.

Her long dress catches on the wind as she walks up the driveway and stumbles.

What the hell is Gracie doing here?

My mother turns an unhappy face my way. "I didn't raise you to watch a lady trip. Go to her."

"Mom—"

"Go to her, son. Life is too short." She pats my shoulder before she walks back into the house, and I meet Grace at the bottom of the porch stairs.

Tears pool in her beautiful eyes. "I'm so sorry, Ares. I know how much you loved your dad." She wraps her arms around my waist and presses her face against my chest. "I came to talk to you this morning, and Caitlin told me what happened."

I pull her against me and rest my chin on her head, so fucking confused about why she's here at all but also strangely relieved she came. "Why were you coming to talk?"

"We don't have to talk about it today," she tells me once she lifts her face to look at me. "But I need you to know I'm here for you."

"Might as well talk about it today, Grace. This entire day is basically an exercise in reminding us all that no one is guaranteed a tomorrow."

She pulls back without dropping her hold on me and goddamn, I missed this woman.

"I needed to tell you I love you. I should have said it before. I should have told you every day."

The hurt, angry part of my brain wants to tell her it's too little, too late, but it could never be too late for us. We were always going to be the endgame.

"And I turned down the Philadelphia Ballet. I also had a long talk with Brynn and Callen and Maddox. I realize I'm a people pleaser, and as ridiculous as it sounds—because seriously, what adult other than me needs to be told this—but I have to think of myself first. My wants. My needs. And learn to prioritize everyone else's after that."

I'm not sure she even realizes she's doing it, but her thumbs are tracing circles under my shirt, and it feels so good to have her hands on me.

"And I'm going to talk to my family too. I'm going to tell them everything. I mean, Nixon already knows."

"Nixon knows what?"

"Everything." She smiles sadly up at me. "I told him the basics this morning and then filled him in on the rest on the plane. I need you to know that I've wanted to come talk to you for days, but I had the flu. And I'm so sorry about your dad, Ares. My heart is breaking for your whole family. But I also need you to know that when I knocked on your door this morning, I had no clue about your dad. My coming to you had nothing to do with what happened. I just finally hadn't spent the entire morning throwing up, so I figured I'd test my luck."

I try to find words, but they fail me.

"I understand if you don't trust me yet. I wouldn't really blame you. But I promise I'm working on it. I know I put everyone else's feelings in front of my own and yours, and I wish I could say I'll never do that again. But I can't make that promise. What I can promise is that I'll try to do better. I promise to love you, and I will do everything I can to put you and me first. I promise to be honest, and I promise never to ask you to lie for me again."

"Grace . . ." I tuck her hair behind her ear, then pull her little white cardigan closed over her black sundress. She feels smaller than she did just weeks ago, and she didn't have anything extra to lose. "Have you gone to the doctor?"

"I did. I went this morning before we came here. See?" She smiles up at me with a sad smile. "I'm taking care of myself. There's a virus going around. I just have to ride it out, for the most part. But they gave me anti-nausea pills. They seem to help."

I hold her so damn close to me and press my lips to her head. So fucking relieved to have her here. To know she's ready to start taking her life in her own hands. "You know, I told my dad about you last week. Told him I was in love with you. And do you know what he said?"

She shakes her head and buries her face in my chest, completely clueless of the strength she's giving me right now.

"He told me I was named after the goddamned god of war. And that love was the only thing in the world worth fighting for."

She presses her lips to the center of my chest, then looks up at me with tears pooling in those big aqua eyes. "I'm sorry it took me so long to fight for us, god of war."

"I'm sorry I left, baby." I lift her chin with my finger and brush my lips over hers.

"Ares . . ." Everly's voice carries from the door.

Shit. Guess she knows now.

GRACE

~~~~

I press my lips to Ares's one more time.

"She's standing behind us, right?" Even knowing she's there doesn't scare me the way it would have weeks ago. Not when I'm in Ares's arms, after being unsure I'd ever get to be here again.

"Yeah, baby." He runs his big hand over my head and down my hair.

"I love you, god of war," I whisper before I turn to face her. "Hey, sissy. How are the kids and Cross?"

My beautiful sister is standing at the top of the steps, confusion clearly written on her face. "Well, Gracie, they're heartbroken. Everyone is. But not everyone is kissing my sister. Want to get your hands off her, god of war?"

Ares brushes his lips over my ear. "I'll play nice if you need me to and go inside because I love you, baby. But don't you dare leave, got it?"

I could cry with how happy his words make me. It's like being bathed in the sun after standing in the dark for too long.

"I'm done playing nice." I slide my hand into his and hold

my ground. "I'm so sorry, Evie. I never wanted you to find out this way. But now really isn't the time to deal with everything. Can we fight about this later?"

Her eyes lock on our joined hands like a heat-seeking missile.

"I'm sorry, *what*? We *don't* argue. You and I never argue. What are you even talking about? What didn't you want me to find out? And why the hell is he holding your hand?"

"Everly." Cross steps out onto the porch, and my heart sinks. "What's going on?"

I'm pretty sure this is what Callen would call a shit show.

"Your brother was just kissing my sister."

Cross looks down at us, confused.

"Seriously. We don't need to do this now. You guys just need to get through the week. I'll go back to the hotel with Nixon," I tell them, not wanting to make any of what Ares and his family are dealing with any harder than it already is.

"Nixon is here?" my sister asks.

At the same time, Ares squeezes my hand in his. "You're not staying in a hotel."

One day, I'll tell him how those words helped heal my broken heart.

"She's not?" Cross asks, then the screen door opens behind him, and Bellamy walks out.

"I've got warm banana bread, if anyone wants some." She looks around, and where I'm expecting to see exhaustion or confusion, there's a smile.

"Took you long enough, good twin. Try not to let him go this time." She lifts the plate a little higher. "Banana bread?"

"No, thank you," I tell her as my stomach rolls, and my sister's head looks like it's about to blow.

"What the hell is happening?" Everly's eyes ping around like a pinball between us all before landing on Bellamy.

"What do you mean it took her long enough?" Everly turns to Cross. "This time? When was last time?"

But Cross isn't confused.

He's pissed.

He kisses Everly's temple and walks back into the house.

"Ares." I tug his hand until he looks down at me. "We don't have to do this now. I can leave."

He frames my face in his hands, not giving a shit that both our sisters are watching us. "You know how you're always doing things for everyone else, and how you're going to make us a priority?"

I nod and soak in the warmth of his hands.

"I need you to do that now. I need you here with me, beautiful. I need to be selfish right now. And I really don't want to have to give a shit how that makes your sister feel. Not today. Not this week."

"Then I'm not going anywhere." I turn my face against his hand and press a kiss to his palm. "Except maybe to walk a little with Evie, so I can talk to her without the argument I know is coming happening on your front lawn."

"Baby, you look like a strong wind could blow you away. Don't go anywhere."

"You're going to have to trust me."

His stormy eyes skim over my face. "I'll be inside. Call if you need me, okay?"

"I'm always going to need you, Ares. These last two weeks were hell without you." The words are soft, but the truth in them is so powerful. "And I'll never stop trying to make up for how long it took me to realize that."

"Just stay with me. That's all I need." He kisses me again quickly and walks past Everly, then presses a palm to Bellamy's back. "Let's leave them alone."

Everly's eyes are practically spitting fire at him as he

walks into the house. "You better start talking now, Gracie. Because I'm about to lose my shit."

I walk up the steps past her and sit on a rocker, so I can fish through my purse and find a piece of the ginger candy I bought at the airport. "Are you going to be loud, Evie? Because if you are, we need to go somewhere else. I didn't come here to make a scene or make anything harder on anyone."

I brace for the conversation I'm least ready to have. This will be the worst one. I know Mom and Dad will be hard too, but Evie . . . this is going to be worse.

"I didn't know you were coming at all." She sits down in the seat across from me and frowns. "What else do I not know, Grace?"

"So many things . . ."

"Care to elaborate? We've got nothing but time." Everly crosses her legs and waits, clearly willing to wait me out. Hope she's just as willing to listen.

My bravado falters as I look at my twin. I hate the idea of hurting her. But I hate the idea of hurting Ares as much, if not more. And it's time I put him first. "I'm in love with Ares. I have been for months."

She opens her mouth, but I refuse to let her stop me now. "He's been the one good thing in my life . . . *just about the only good thing* since I moved to London."

"You mean since you *came home* from London."

I shake my head, gently. "No, Evie. Since I moved. I was miserable there."

"What?" That one word . . . four little letters, they hold so much pain. "How did I not know?"

"Because I never told you." I've got to own this if I'm going to move forward. "I went out of my way to make sure you never found out because I didn't want to hurt you or Mom and Dad. I didn't want anyone to be disappointed in me. And maybe, deep down, I thought you knew me better than I knew myself."

"Grace." She reaches out and takes my hand. "I don't understand."

"Why would you, when I never shared how unhappy I was with anyone?"

"But Ares knew?"

"He saw it before I did. I just didn't want to believe him." This man . . . the one who, even an ocean away, knew I was unhappy and forced me to face my feelings. "Ballet hasn't made me happy in a really long time, but I was so scared of failure. Of letting everyone down. Of having to figure out what my life looked like without ballet in it."

She drops my hand and narrows her eyes. "Have I ever made you feel like you couldn't tell me? Have I ever told you dancing was more important than *you* are? I'm struggling to understand why you would feel more comfortable talking to *him* about any of this than you would talking to *me*. To Mom. We're your *family*. We know what ballet is like."

"Because deep down, this isn't about you or Mom or even Ares. This is about me and my need to please the people around me more than I ever bothered to take care of myself. And it's also about Ares—because he saw that. He saw me. The real me. *The broken me.* And he loved me anyway. And he forced me to open my eyes and see it too."

"You realize this is insane, right? Ares . . . the god of war? He what . . . fixed you?" She laughs bitterly, and I'm not sure I've ever been so mad at my sister before.

"He's a manwhore, Grace." Okay. Point made. Because now my anger just turned to rage. "He doesn't take anything seriously. Why, if he loves you so much, were you lying to your family about being in a relationship with him?"

"Listen, I know I fucked up, and I'm owning it. But if you say that about him again, we're going to go from me feeling bad for hurting you to us having a whole different problem. That man is no whore. And if you seriously believe any of the bullshit you just spewed, you really don't know him at all."

The wood beneath my nails digs into my skin from how tightly I'm holding onto the rocker, trying to keep my anger in check and my words quiet and even.

"Also, he didn't fix me. He forced me to see what I didn't want to recognize, and then instead of trying to fix it for me —like everyone else has done for me my entire life—he told me I had to fix it myself and then forced my hand. If he hadn't, I would never have taken any steps to be happier."

She doesn't look like she believes a word I'm saying, but I'm starting to realize that's *her* problem to work through. Not mine.

"What exactly does being happier look like?" Her words are callous and so unlike my sister, I know I've struck a nerve and she's hitting back. And I can't blame her.

My actions started this, and now we all have to deal with the fallout in some way.

"I turned down the offer to dance in Philadelphia."

"What?" She smacks the arm rest, and I wince at the anger behind that word. "That was the perfect job for you, and it kept you close."

"Here's the thing, I need you to think about what you just said. Because your version of the perfect job and mine are two very different things at this point. And again, I take part of the blame for this. You couldn't have known how much I don't want to dance anymore—because I didn't tell you. I hid how badly I was hurting. How numb I was to everything else. And I did that because I didn't want anyone to worry about me. But you should have been worried. I was miserable. I was in pain. I'm pretty sure I was one step away from being sexually harassed by my director. And I didn't tell anyone. But

THE KNOCKOUT

now I'm done, Evie. I'm done dancing professionally. At least as a ballerina."

With matching tears pooling in our eyes, she swallows down her emotions and stares at me like she doesn't know me at all. "But he saw all that? You let him see—but not me?"

"I didn't actually realize I was letting him see anything. He just forced his way in and refused to leave. Refused to let me keep hurting. But I didn't want to hear it. Hear him. You're not the only stubborn Sinclair, you know."

She slowly shakes her head, taking in everything I've said. "Do you know your next move?"

"I do. I'm going to choreograph Lilah's show and hire and train her dancers. And I get to do all of that from Kroydon Hills. It's my version of a dream job. *My new dream.*" I sit a little taller, excited about this next step.

"And Ares?"

"He's the love of my life." My tone leaves no room for argument, but Evie's still gonna try.

"The god of war? Are you sure?"

I'm not sure if she's serious, but I don't care. "I'm positive."

"Does anybody else know?"

I shrug and close my eyes as I lean back in the rocker. "I think so."

Bellamy steps outside with a little tray and three cups of tea. "I know. Caitlin knows. According to what you said earlier, Nixon knows too. And I'm pretty sure Brynlee knows something. Maddox and Callen are pretty clueless, but I think they have an idea something is going on."

When Everly and I both look at her, she smiles and leans back against the railing, facing us. "Did you really not see the open window between the two of you?"

We both turn and look at the screened window open

behind the table between us, then turn back to Bellamy in slow motion.

"What? Like we weren't all in there listening? Cross and Ares heard most of it before Cross stormed off into the backyard and Ares followed him. That's when I decided it was safe to join you guys."

"Cross stormed off?" Evie asks.

"Ares followed him?" I add.

The three of us stay quiet for a minute, then follow the sound of angry male voices.

Shit.

Ares

"You had to go for Gracie? My. Wife's. Sister." Cross turns on me, furious. "What . . . you fucked your way through the rest of Philadelphia and decided you needed someone respectable, so you might as well go for Everly's twin?"

Listening to my woman stand up for herself should have been a good thing, but instead, my brother has somehow twisted it into something else. Something darker.

"What the fuck, man? It's not like I'm some evil mastermind with a devious plan to steal away the quiet little virgin."

Cross's nostrils flare, and for a minute, I think we're going to throw down the way we used to as teenagers.

"That's my wife's family you're fucking with, Ares. Her family. My family. You hurt her—you hurt Everly. And I'm not going to let that happen."

I think about hitting him.

I really do.

It would feel good too . . . for about a minute.

But the last thing in the world Mom needs or Dad would have wanted is for Cross and me to come to blows in their back yard. "The fuck? Do you know me at all, asshole?"

The girls walk around the corner of the house, and I try to reel it in.

But man, it's fucking hard.

"Did anyone assume you were going to hurt Everly? Or did we all give you the space you needed to figure your shit out?"

"You're not me, Ares. You're never going to be me. Stop trying."

"I'll give you that one today—for Dad. But say it again and see what happens."

"Hey," Gracie snaps and runs over to me. "He doesn't need to be you." She slides under my arm and wraps her arms around my waist.

"Don't be a dick, Cross," Bellamy adds as she comes to my rescue. "He's just as much of a good man as you are."

Everly's the last to walk over—a little slower than the other two. And she's staring at me like it's the first time she's ever seen me before she carefully maneuvers herself between Cross and Grace. "Leave him alone, Cross. He loves my sister."

"Hurt her and I'll kill you," he threatens me. And I respect it.

"I can take care of myself, Cross," Gracie whispers.

I tighten my grip on her. "But you'll never have to because I'll kill anyone who ever hurts you."

"If you boys have spent enough time threatening each other, I'd like to go to bed now," Mom calls from the back door.

Cross and I don't say anything, but Bellamy runs over and kisses Mom.

"Thank you for coming up, Gracie. You can sleep in Bellamy's bed if you'd like to spend the night tonight."

"Mom," I groan. "Really?"

"I didn't say she had to sleep *with* Bellamy, dear. We upgraded Bellamy's bed a few years ago, and it's bigger than yours. Figure it out with your sister." Then she turns around, leaving us all staring as she goes.

"I am not sleeping in your bed, Ares," Bellamy whines.

"The couch works too," Cross offers, and we all laugh, breaking the tension and heavy emotion we've been walking blindly through all day.

Gracie nuzzles in closer. "I've got a big bed back at the hotel."

"You're not staying at the hotel. Family doesn't stay at the hotel," Cross tells Grace as Everly walks into his arms.

"Nixon's at the hotel," Everly pipes up.

"Maybe *I* should go to the hotel," Bellamy mumbles, and all eyes fly to her. "Oh my God. I didn't mean it like that."

"If you tell me you're banging my brother, I'm going to barf," Everly giggles, and Gracie gags.

"You okay, baby?" I bend my knees to look at her, and Grace's face turns a little green—right before she *actually* throws up.

GRACE

"My mom said to drink this." Ares sets a cup of ginger tea on the night stand next to me and brushes my damp hair away from my face. "How are you feeling?"

The last burst of the setting sun filters through the curtains and lights up his handsome face. Golden and shimmering and bringing me peace on a day that should have seen me giving it to him.

"Better," I admit. "The shower helped." I relax back against Bellamy's pillows, and a possessive wave washes over his face when he realizes what I'm wearing.

"Are those the sweats I gave you last winter?" He sits next to me and carefully pulls me to him until I slide my leg over his lap and straddle him. "I like my name on you, Grace."

"Me too," I whisper, still so grateful I'm here. With him. "I slept in these all last winter," I admit quietly.

His eyes fill with a beautiful lusty haze, and his hands slide under my hoodie. "Thanks for coming back to me, beautiful."

"Thanks for waiting for me," I whisper back against his

lips and gently rock against his hard dick. Ares's fingers dig into my ass, and a hot, heavy shot of need races through my blood. "I might get you sick."

"I don't fucking care," he tells me, then lifts my arms over my head and pulls the sweatshirt off, then helps me shimmy out of the sweats and my panties as he shucks off his boxers. It's a well-timed balancing act that promises the best reward when I'm back in his lap and gloriously naked seconds later.

Ares traces his tongue along the hollow of my neck. "I missed the taste of your skin."

"I need you," I gasp as the head of his cock nestles against my core.

Both big hands slide over my ass and pull me against him until he's settled between my thighs, and a breathless moan leaves my lips. "Please . . ." My pussy throbs with an overwhelming need in sync with the beat of my heart. And when he finally pushes inside me, it's like the world around us settles and snaps back into place.

Our movements aren't rushed or frenzied.

They're slow and lazy. Measured and tender.

We're quiet and careful. Aware of the full house around us.

It's a dance. The kind I can lose myself in.

His kiss leaves me dying for more, and I wonder silently how I ever lived without him, vowing to never do it again. I wrap my legs around his waist, leaving no room between us. My nails drag down his back, and his hard body rubs against my soft skin.

I lean back and brace my hands on his thighs, leaving myself completely at his mercy, and the sweetest sigh slips past my lips as one arm wraps around my back.

"I've got you, baby."

It's us.

It's only ever been us, and it's only ever going to be us.

This man. This life. I want him. I want it.

When my orgasm finally rolls over me like a warm ocean wave dragging me under, it's with his name on my lips and a promise to love him forever.

I realize just how lucky I've been as I'm getting ready for Ares's father's funeral two days later. I've been to so few funerals in my life, I had no idea how this all worked. While I'm standing in the bathroom in my black dress, touching up my waterproof mascara, Ares walks in with my phone in his hand.

"Looks like urgent care is calling you."

"Can you hit speaker for me?" He nods, and I answer, "Hello?"

"Grace Sinclair?" the faceless voice asks from the other end of the phone.

"This is she." *Shit.* I just stabbed myself in the eye.

"I'm calling with the bloodwork panel you had done during your visit. Were you aware you're eight weeks pregnant?"

My mascara hits the white marble counter and bounces to the floor as I wrap my hands around the sink in an attempt not to fall. Then I see Ares's reflection through the mirror. We're both in shock.

"I'm sorry. Could you repeat that?" I ask because there's no way I just heard them right, *right*?

"These blood tests are pretty accurate. It appears you're eight weeks pregnant. The anti-nausea medication we prescribed yesterday is safe to continue to take as needed, but we recommend you follow up with your ob-gyn. Losing as much weight as you've lost isn't safe for you or the baby. They'll be better equipped to help you handle your condition."

"Condition," I repeat as a hysterical laugh gets caught in my throat.

"Doctor Peters believes it's hyperemesis gravidarum. Your OB will be able to go into more detail. But in the meantime, you need to rest and stay hydrated. If your vomit becomes discolored or bloody, please go right to the hospital."

Ares picks up the phone and holds it between us as he asks, "What do you mean discolored? It's puke. Isn't it always discolored?"

His hand wraps around my neck and squeezes, and I hadn't realized I was holding my breath until that moment when it wooshes out of me.

"Brown or tinged with blood. Do you have any other questions, Ms. Sinclair?"

I stare at the phone in his hand and lose focus.

"We'll make the appointment. Thank you." Ares hangs up the phone and sits me on the counter next to my mascara. "Baby . . ." he whispers, and I force myself to focus on him. "You're scaring me, Grace."

"Good. Because I'm pretty fucking scared too. I can't be pregnant. My life is a mess. I don't have a job. I don't have health insurance. I was proud of myself because I had a job with my cousin Lilah lined up, and I got you back. My biggest accomplishment today was that I only puked twice."

"Well, that's good," he tells me, trying to be supportive.

"It's only eight a.m.," I whisper. "Give it time."

"A baby," he whispers and presses his lips to my forehead. "You're having our baby."

My head spins, and my world tilts. "You're not mad?"

"No, Grace. I'm so far from mad, I'm in another galaxy." He drops to his knee, and I kick him in the chest.

"I swear to God, Ares Wilder. If you drop to your knee and propose right now, I will withhold sex one year for every second it takes for you to stand back up."

He jumps up to his feet, and I smile at him—not quite a laugh but definitely a smile.

"How are we going to do this?" How is he not losing his mind when internally, I'm screaming and shaking in a corner?

"The same way we do everything else. Together," he assures me. I half expect him to laugh after that, but he doesn't. He just cups my face in his hands. "Do you love me, Grace?"

I nod, unable to say anything.

"Do you want to marry me one day?"

"Yeah." I smile again, and his sexy smile shines back.

"Then we'll figure it out. It was going to happen one day anyway. What difference does the order make?"

"Really?" I reach for him and straighten his tie. "It's just that simple for you?"

"Baby, before you got here last night, I was thinking about the fact that my dad would never know you as my wife. He'd never meet our kids. And now, on the day we're going to lay him to rest, we find this out? I kinda feel like it's a gift from him."

Ares

You never know what real strength is until it's tested.

I'll never measure strength by the power of

my fists again—because real strength is standing by your mother's side all day as we say our final goodbyes to the greatest father I could ever have. The man who gave me my love of hockey. Who showed me what a man is and how he loves. Real strength is in the legacy you leave behind at the end of the day.

I slide my hand into Grace's as we step from the limo out into the sun at my parents' house, where the luncheon has been set up outside.

She hasn't talked to her family about anything yet. Everly and Nixon are the only ones who know about us or her decision about ballet. And it's obvious from the looks we've been receiving all day, the questions are coming.

She and I carefully and slowly move into the backyard. She's been queasy all morning. And the faster she moves, the worse it seems to get.

"Oh, Ares, honey." Annabelle wraps me up in a big hug as soon as we get close enough, and Declan kisses the top of Grace's head. "We're so sorry. Your father seemed like one of a kind."

"Thank you. He was." I shake Declan's hand and watch a small smile tug at the corners of his mouth as his wife hugs their daughter. He pulls me against him. "If you break her heart, I will kill you," he whispers, and I look up at him, wondering if he realizes how fucked up those words are today. But then I think about if the roles were reversed and that was my daughter.

"I'll protect it with my life," I tell him just as quietly.

"Good man." He pats my back, and I'm pretty sure I just got Grace's dad's blessing.

Might change his mind, though, when he finds out she's pregnant.

Grace kisses my cheek. "I'm going to go inside and get a drink. Do you want anything?"

"Why don't you let me get that?" I offer, but she shakes her head.

"You know these people. You need to go talk to them. I'll be okay."

I watch her walk away and miss her touch immediately.

GRACE

〜

I stand in Ares's mother's quiet living room and study the walls filled with family pictures. Birthdays. Graduations. A Christmas spent with Bellamy in a hospital bed with teenage Cross and Ares on either side of her. It's a wall of love. Of memories. And there's a picture with Ares and a beautiful young woman decked out in a tux and gown that I'm guessing is from a prom. Even as a teenager, the early makings of my god of war are written all over his handsome face.

"That one was his senior prom," his mom walks up behind me, and I jump. "Sorry. I didn't mean to startle you."

I can't imagine the kind of pain she's in right now, and I feel helpless to do anything. "No. I'm fine. Can I get you anything?"

She lifts the picture from the hook it hangs on and traces Ares's face with the tip of her finger. "He looks the most like his father."

"He does," I agree with a smile and find myself wondering if our baby will look like Ares or me.

"Hey, beautiful." Speak of the devil. He drops a kiss on my

head, then runs his hand over his mother's back. "Do you need anything, Momma?"

"I need everyone to stop fussing over me. Today is a celebration of your father's life and the legacy he leaves behind. Not his death. He lives on in each of you kids." She hands me the picture, then looks outside and wipes an errant tear from her eye. "I better get back outside. Gracie, honey, if you don't feel well, you should go lie down."

"I will, thank you." I wait until she leaves and smile at the picture in my hands. "Wanna tell me who this is and if I should be jealous?" I tease.

But Ares doesn't smile, and I immediately worry that I shouldn't have joked today.

He takes the picture from my hands and studies it for a minute. "Sarah was a girl I dated in high school. You know, when you think you know everything there is to know about the world and what life is going to be like. Really, I didn't know anything."

"Hey," I move into his chest, sensing this is hitting a nerve I hadn't realized was exposed. "I'm sorry. We don't need to talk about it."

"She's why I hate liars," he says the words so carefully, it's almost like he's saying them to himself and not me. At least until he looks at me and cups my face in his hand. "She's why I hate drugs too. She was a gymnast and tore her ACL our senior year. It's terrible how easily someone can become addicted to pain killers and how fast that can snowball."

The final piece of the puzzle clicks into place, and my heart sinks. "Ares . . . I'm so sorry. Did she get help?"

"She did. Her parents were amazing. They never stopped trying to help her. But she struggled for years. Last I heard, she was a few years sober and getting her degree in drug counseling."

"You know that's not me, right?" I ask, needing to get him out of the past and back to the present.

"It could have been though."

I lift up on my toes and press my lips to his. "But it's not. I'm right here. I haven't touched my prescription since London, months ago. I'm okay."

"Yeah, baby. I know." He drops to his knees and presses his lips to my stomach. "Now I just need to keep you both that way."

"What are you—" Bellamy starts, but Everly cuts her off.

"Are you kidding me?" She shoves Ares out of the way and presses her hands on my flat stomach. "Are you pregnant?"

I'm not sure if I want to cry or scream or maybe laugh. I just got him back. Just changed my entire life and had the hardest conversations I've ever had with the two people I love most in the world before I found out I was pregnant. Was it really too much to ask the universe for a day or two to get used to the idea of a baby before everyone else found out?

"What the hell, blondie?" Ares grumbles as he gets up, and Cross laughs.

"Might as well get used to this shit. These two talk almost every night. Grace was in my bed more than I was during the season."

Everly looks at Ares, who I'm pretty sure is thinking dirty, dirty thoughts. "Get your mind out of the gutter, god of war. He means FaceTime." Apparently, that's what she's thinking too.

"Oh, just wait," I tell them both. "It'll be worse now that I'm home for good."

"Yeah? Everly could be in our bed?" Ares asks with the damn sexy smirk.

"Our bed. I like it." I kiss him.

Cross growls, "Without my wife."

"Who's talking about your wife?" Ares blows him off, and I want to kiss him again.

"Oh my God. You could come stay with me when the guys are gone for away games. We can get fat and pregnant together," Everly says.

"Wait . . . Who's pregnant?" Bellamy asks, and I laugh and reach for Ares's hand.

Without another word, she turns to walk away.

"Hey," Ares yells out. "Where are you going? We haven't told anyone yet."

"I'm not saying a word. I'm just getting the hell out of here, in case it's contagious."

Hours later, with my head resting against the wall, and my arms in my new favorite spot wrapped around the toilet, Ares walks in with a ginger ale and a smile. "So I was thinking . . ."

"Hasn't anyone ever told you you're not supposed to do that?" I tease with what little energy I have left.

"Listen, I thought our parents handled the whole pregnancy thing pretty well. But I think we got off easy on the questions, since it was already a shit day. I want to have answers for them and for us."

It turned out, Bellamy didn't need to tell or not tell anyone anything. Momma Wilder was in the kitchen while we were talking and heard everything, and we decided we couldn't let one parent know and not the others. I still need to have the full-blown, breakdown conversation with my parents. But in light of everything happening, that's going to have to wait until we get back to Kroydon Hills.

"Okay, shoot. What answers have you come up with while my head has been in a toilet?" I stretch my legs out in front of me and watch Ares's stormy eyes go molten hot as my dress slides up high on my thigh.

"I think we should buy a house close to Cross and Everly. That way the two of you have each other when Cross and I are on the road. The hockey season is long as fuck, baby. And you're going to need help."

I tilt my head to the side and bite down on my lip. "Okay, Wilder, I'm trying to follow where you're going with this, but you lost me."

He flips his phone around and shows me a picture of the house next to Cross and Everly's.

"The Vicolis live there. That house isn't for sale."

He takes his phone back and shoves it in his pocket before he reaches down and picks me up. "Let me worry about that."

I wrap my arms around his neck and rest my head against his chest. "You know, we haven't even discussed moving in together. I think we're skipping some steps."

"Marry me, Grace."

I laugh and pat his chest. "I told you not to ask me that today."

"Fine. Then move in with me."

I manage not to say *fuck no* and settle for, "I'm not living with my brother again."

"Then I'll move in with you." He says it so matter-of-factly, I smile.

"It's not my condo. I'll have to ask Brynn."

"She likes me. It'll be fine."

I want to laugh, but my stomach is too uneasy to risk it. Instead, I settle in against him. "I do like the idea of living near Everly and Cross." The idea of raising our babies together makes me want to cry, but I've felt like that a lot over the past few days.

He carries me into the bedroom and lays me down on the bed.

"Stay with me," I whisper and take his hand in mine.

"Forever, baby." He climbs in bed behind me and pulls me against his chest.

"I love you, good twin."

"Until the end of time, god of war. Until the end of time."

EPILOGUE

ARES

She's not the song you dance to. She's the lyrics you can't get out of your head.
—Ares's secret thoughts

"Remind me why we didn't hire movers?" Cross and I lift up the couch that Callen and Nixon just took off the truck, and they all fucking stare at me like I'm stupid. Which I might be. Because at some point, I must have thought this was a good idea.

"Dude. Because we're men. We don't need to hire people when we can do it ourselves." Cross kinda grunts, and I just shake my fucking head.

"Listen, I know I wanna be you and all that shit, but next time let me be the smarter Wilder and hire someone to do this."

"Come on. You're never gonna let me live that down, are you?" he bitches, and I laugh.

"Nope. Never letting you live that down. Why do you

think I bought the house next to yours? I want to be you, man. Same street. Same team. Twin wives," I tease.

"She hasn't said yes yet," Callen fucking cackles from next to us, and I accidentally elbow him while we're walking up the steps.

"She's going to say yes." If all goes as planned, she might even say yes *tonight*.

It only takes us a few hours to get everything moved in. Grace's mom and aunts are basically rockstars, who get it all unpacked and cleaned up as we go, while our twin pregnant princesses sit on the newly placed couch with their feet up.

I'm standing in the backyard, watching Cross chase the kids around and looking out at my view of the lake, wondering if Dad would have liked it as much as his view of the ocean, when Declan walks up to me and hands me a beer. "She looks happy in there."

I look through the wall of windows into the family room and see my girl laughing with her mom and sister. Everyone else has left for the night. "That's my goal."

"You know, you kids hit us with a lot of things all at once over the summer, and I'm not gonna lie and say we were happy about all of it. When they're babies, it's so easy to protect them from everything and keep them in this safe bubble. Then they grow up and force you to let go. And in a lot of ways, Gracie let us hang on just a little bit more than Evie. Always my careful girl. My easy girl. The one her mother and I knew would be happy and healthy and fulfilled. Finding out she wasn't. That she hadn't been . . . It's a fucking humbling thing when you realize you're not the one who knows what's best for your kids. And then to find out it was another man who helped her. Who loves her . . ."

He grabs my shoulder and squeezes. "Who knocked her up. Well . . . it's not an easy thing. But at the end of the day, you hope when they fall in love and start a life, it's with a good man. A man like you, Ares. I saw it that day on the beach. The way the two of you watched each other. Annabelle did too. We talked about it the whole ride back to Kroydon Hills that night. We hoped we were right. Belles and I did things a little out of order too, and we've been happy for over twenty-five years. Hopefully, you'll be able to say the same."

"Seriously, Dec. I don't know what to say. I love her. She's my life."

"And that's all you need to say, kid. But I've got to ask one thing . . . did you really think through moving the girls in next door to each other? You and Cross are going to get bitched at in stereo. They have a borg mind. Piss one off, you piss them both off. Good luck with that."

"Thanks," I laugh. Pretty fucking sure the good is going to outweigh the bad.

"What are you doing, Ares? I can't see."

"You're blindfolded, good twin. That's kind of the plan." I steer her through the house and onto the wraparound porch, facing the lake and waterfalls behind us. "Bend your knees, baby."

"What?" She laughs.

"Bend and sit," I tell her and hold her arms as she moves super slowly. My girl is five months pregnant with the next set of Sinclair twins, who happen to be the first set of Wilder twins. One boy and one girl.

I untie her blindfold. "Okay, baby. Open your eyes."

Her aqua eyes open slowly and take in the white wooden

rocker she's sitting in, then over at the matching one next to it. "Ares . . ."

"I figured we could sit out here and have coffee in the mornings and enjoy our view."

Tears trickle down her face. Pregnancy has definitely made her more of a crier, and she was already one to start with. "Just like your mom and dad."

I drop down on one knee and crack open the Tiffany box with the brilliant-cut diamond nestled inside. "Grace Sinclair . . . I love you with everything I am and ever will be. I want to spend my life loving you and our babies. I know I'm not a perfect man. But I promise to be the best man I can be, if you'll let me."

She covers her face with her hands, then peeks through her fingers, crying. "Ares . . ."

"Baby, I'm begging you, put me out of my misery and say yes."

She nods her head and very carefully tries to throw herself into my arms. "I love you, Ares."

"Until the end of time, baby."

The End

Want more Gracie & Ares?
Download their extended epilogue!

Download the extended epilogue here

The Philly Press

KROYDON KRONICLES

NOT READY TO SAY GOODBYE YET?

Looks like our favorite Kroydon Hills socialites are at it one last time! *The Sweet Spot*, the final book in the Playing To Win series, is releasing this summer.

Stay tuned to see who's next...

Preorder The Sweet Spot Now

#KroydonKronicles #TheSweetSpot

WHAT COMES NEXT?

If you haven't read the first book in the Kings Of Kroydon Hills series, you can start with *All In* today!

Read All In for FREE on KU

ACKNOWLEDGMENTS

M. ~ Every word I write is because you're my strength.

My dream team, Brianna and Heather ~ Thank you for all that you do to keep my world spinning while I hide in my cave and get lost in Kroydon Hills. I am forever grateful.

Dena ~ We did it! I keep saying one of these days I will get back on schedule. Here's hoping it happens with the next book.

To the incredible women who read every word many, many, many times before this book was ready to be published, Jenn, Tammy, Bri, Heather, Vicki, & Kelly ~ Thank you from the very bottom of my heart. I am so lucky to have you in my corner and to count you as my friends.

For all of my Jersey Girls ~ Thank you for giving me a safe space and showing me so much grace.

To all of the Indie authors out there who have helped me along the way – you are amazing! This community is so incredibly supportive, and I am so lucky to be a part of it.

Thank you to all of the bloggers who took the time to read, review, and promote The Knockout.

And finally, the biggest thank you to you, the reader. To

those of you who have been with me since Gracie's parents' book was published three years ago and those of you have just stumbled onto the world of Kroydon Hills now, I hope you've enjoyed reading Gracie and Ares as much as I have loved writing them.

ABOUT THE AUTHOR

Bella Matthews is a USA Today & Amazon Top 11 Bestselling author. She is married to her very own Alpha Male and raising three little ones. You can typically find her running from one sporting event to another. When she is home, she is usually hiding in her home office with the only other female in her house, her rescue dog Tinker Bell by her side. She likes to write swoon-worthy heroes and sassy, smart heroines. Sarcasm is her love language and big family dynamics are her favorite thing to add to each story.

Stay Connected

Amazon Author Page: https://amzn.to/2UWU7Xs
Facebook Page: https://www.facebook.com/bella.matthews.3511
Reader Group: https://www.facebook.com/groups/599671387345008/
Instagram: https://www.instagram.com/bellamatthews.author/
Bookbub: https://www.bookbub.com/authors/bella-matthews
Goodreads: https://www.goodreads.com/.../show/20795160.Bella_Matthews
TikTok: https://vm.tiktok.com/ZMdfNfbQD/
Newsletter: https://bit.ly/BMNLsingups
Patreon: https://www.patreon.com/BellaMatthews

ALSO BY BELLA MATTHEWS

Kings of Kroydon Hills
All In
More Than A Game
Always Earned, Never Given
Under Pressure

Restless Kings
Rise of the King
Broken King
Fallen King

The Risks We Take Duet
Worth The Risk
Worth The Fight

Defiant Kings
Caged
Shaken
Iced
Overruled
Haven

Playing To Win
The Keeper
The Wildcat
The Knockout

The Sweet Spot

CHECK OUT BELLA'S WEBSITE

Scan the QR code or go to http://authorbellamatthews.com
to stay up to date with all things Bella Matthews

Printed in Great Britain
by Amazon